INVADER OF
THE CANAL WORLD

When I had first seen this planet big and clear on the scopes, I had jokingly suggested calling it Barsoom. Since then, in some ways, that had proved quite appropriate: canals, red men, even a few fierce warriors . . . And I was going to meet a queen—the queen of an ancient, beautiful, proud city. Perhaps I could fascinate her, sweep her off her feet, become a Xuman prince. Tom Carson, the Warlord of Yelsai . . .

Crap.

I wasn't cut out for that sort of act. I didn't feel in the slightest like a hero, and I wasn't one. I wasn't going to marry any red princess if I could avoid it . . . What was I, really? An invader—a bumbling invader, my whole heroism packed into my hip holster. My mission here was Plan 2/3/A —otherwise known as *divide and rule* . . . Once we had shown the Queen what we could do, we would offer her the empire of her whole world—literally —on condition that she make over to us a reasonable slice of it. . . .

But a civilization that had lasted two million years was just not that simple.

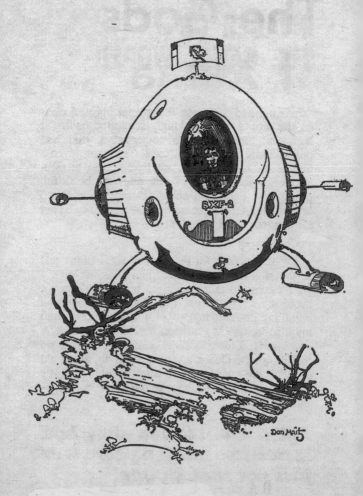

BXF-2

Don Marts

The Gods of Xuma

or
Barsoom Revisited

DAVID J. LAKE

DAW BOOKS, INC.

DONALD A. WOLLHEIM, PUBLISHER

1301 Avenue of the Americas
New York, N. Y.   10019

Hamlet: *There's a divinity that shapes our ends . . .*

FIRST PRINTING, FEBRUARY 1978

1 2 3 4 5 6 7 8 9

PRINTED IN U.S.A.

CONTENTS

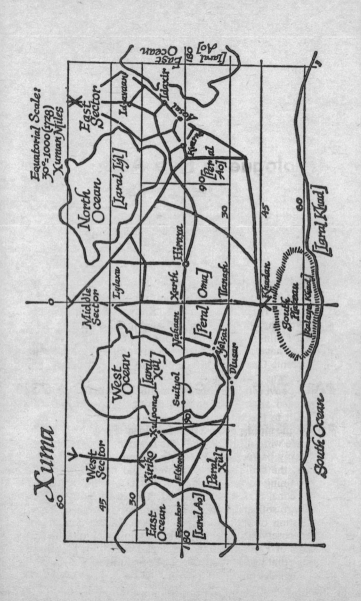

Prologue in Five Acts:

I — The Astronomer

'0-8-4/0-9/0-3. Tonight from the sky tower of the Queen's Palace in Yelsai, I, Kanyo of Xulpona, observed something so unusual among the Whirling Stars that I think it well worth noting down in this private diary. I have already dispatched my official report to the Supreme Ones in Khadan (copy to Queen Telesin), but there was a strangeness about the event which I could not convey in the dryness of official phrasing. It transcended angles, magnitudes, timings. Perhaps if I confide it to this more intimate leaf-of-speech plant, I may become more master of my emotions.

We were on the roof of the tower not long after sunset, my partner and I. At this season of Southern summer, the sun sets south of west, and the red glow was remaining in the direction of the Desert of Death and the canal that leads to Dlusar. The street lights of Yelsai are soft and tastefully shaded, so there could be no question of spurious optical effects. In the dull red of our observers' lantern I could only just pick out the features of Psyl's face; and perhaps I could not even have done that had I not known Psyl's features so well.

She—let me call Psyl "she," as I still do in my heart,

7

though of course my fellow is now an Elder like myself—she was swinging the Belt telescope to follow #1-5, which is a pretty dim Whirler, when suddenly I heard her utter an exclamation. As I looked up from the map table, she said:

"Kanyo, there is a new bright Whirler in the Belt! It must be visible to the naked eye—look—"

She was still peering through the telescope, afraid to lose the object, but I followed the direction of the tube—and there it was! It was certainly a Whirling Star, for it was visibly moving from west to east. From its relative slowness I would have said it was fairly distant, and yet its brightness was extraordinary. Among the Whirlers, I would have placed it slightly brighter than #0-5, or Second Star-Grade as it passed the zenith north of us.

"There is no such Whirler," I said hoarsely. "The brightest we can expect about this hour is Zero-Eight, and that will not be rising yet a while. Yet this one is moving exactly like a Whirler, west to east in the Belt. There it goes now—yes, it will set due east. Ah, it's fading now, but—"

"I can still see it," said Psyl, swinging her tube. "Yes, Kanyo, now . . . it's going into eclipse, still heading for the east point. Gone now." She straightened up, and looked at me.

"It is a change in the Heavens," I said, "like a nova or a comet—but in the *Belt*! Nothing like that has been seen these myriad years. Perhaps some collision—"

"A collision of Whirlers would surely have produced an inclined orbit, my dear," said Psyl. "Besides, I haven't yet told you everything. I saw that new Whirler being born!"

"What? How—"

"I was watching Number 1-5 when suddenly I saw a flare of light at the extreme edge of the field. It was as though someone had lit a bonfire in the sky! Or a burning torch. The flame was moving east, and there was a bright point at its tail. The flame and the point grew brighter as I watched, and then suddenly the flame went out and left the point. That point was the new Whirler, and from then on it was still growing in

8

brightness, but more slowly, as normal Whirlers do when they approach the zenith. Kanyo, if this new one had been in orbit before that flare, I would have observed it much earlier. It just wasn't there! It seemed to come out of deep space, burning, and then falling into a regular orbit."

"Psyl, are you sure—"

"I am sure," she said. "Kanyo, you have trained me well enough to observe accurately. After the flare, that Whirler was in the equatorial orbit. It was in no such orbit before the flare—it was much farther out, and I think coming downwards."

"But Whirlers just don't behave like that," I protested.

"Then maybe this is not really a Whirler." She hesitated. "Kanyo, there is still one thing I haven't told you. All Whirlers look more or less like points, don't they? Well, this one *didn't*. As it passed the zenith, I could just make out a *shape*. It was not a point—it was a tiny rod. It was longer in the direction in which it was travelling."

I shook my head feebly; then I recovered from the shock of these impossibilities.

"Come now, Psyl, all we can do is treat it as a normal Whirler, and work out a rough orbital period, and estimate the size. My guess for the first would be about four hours. When next it passes our meridian—*if* it passes—it will be in eclipse. But at its rising, and again tomorrow evening, we should pick it up. So should the rest of the world, for that matter."

We performed our calculations. The period seemed to be roughly four and a quarter hours; and from Psyl's description the size—the *length*—would be greater than two gross of fathoms, or one-third of a mile.

"If that is right," I said, startled, "it is the biggest Whirler known; bigger even than Number 0-1."

"If it *is* a Whirler," repeated Psyl. "I think . . ."

"What? Go on, my dear."

"A chariot of the gods," she said.

"My dear," I said, taking her in my arms, "if it were the gods, would they come in just one little chariot? Surely not . . ."

9

The red glow had now died in the west. All around us lay the soft lights of Yelsai, and beyond them the blackness of the desert, and above them the enigmatic stars.

II — The Captain

82 Eridani 3 is a planet which has filled some of us with a sense of *déjà vu*. Not that there is any such planet in the home Solar System, nor (as far as we know) in any other actual system. The truth is that it reminds us of a certain *fictitious* planet—one well known in the speculative science and fantastic romances of the early Twentieth Century.

I guess I jumped the countdown a bit. O.K., this is an informal journal tape of Captain Mannheim, of the starship *Riverhorse I,* dated 3/26/2143, home reckoning. All systems go and program nominal as of now. As of now, we are in orbit around 82 Eridani 3, at a distance of one planetary radius from the surface—10,000 kilometers out from the center of mass, a circular equatorial orbit. It's equatorial because this is a coolish planet on the whole, and the equatorial regions are the best ones. There are ice caps at both poles. At present it's Southern summer, and the north ice extends down to about Latitude 45. The south ice comes up to about Latitude 60. The surface is mainly reddish desert, with large depressions in three areas on or north of the Equator—we think they're the beds of dried-up ocean because our instruments tell us they're largely covered with salt deposits. They certainly look pale, yellowish. There are a few lakes at the lowest points of these beds—the remnants of the oceans, I guess. But the former oceans are not the interesting areas.

What's really bugging us is the ice-free "dry land," which is divided by the oceans into three semi-continuous sectors. As I said, these are largely red deserts, but they are crisscrossed by a system of canals. Yes, I repeat, canals! Just like in that old fictitious Mars of the American astronomer Lowell. There is no doubt about this at all; our scopes show clear-cut lines following great circles—they're obviously engineered. The system runs up to the north polar cap in three places, and to the south cap in one. There is one canal which runs almost due north and south from the one cap to the other—we have adopted this as our prime meridian for mapping purposes. About 120 degrees east of this Number One canal the system comes to a climax in the north equatorial region between two of the dried-up oceans. There the desert is crisscrossed with canals—hell, no, it's not desert there, it's bluish-green land, and the instruments are telling us VEGETATION loud and clear. There is another fairly lush area at about 120 West. This planet is not only the abode of life, it must be the abode of *intelligent* life. Contingency Plan-Group 2/3 is therefore in operation.

Oh, ah, one minor problem—nomenclature. We can't go on calling this world 82 Eridani 3; a committee is receiving suggestions at this moment. I have suggested "Ares"—spelt A,R,E,S—the Greek form corresponding to the Roman MARS. I hate to say this, but one joker in our crew—Thomas Carson, our linguist—has suggested BARSOOM. In case the reference is obscure, let me add that this was the name of an even more fictional planet than Lowell's, in some very trashy stories of the Twentieth Century. Carson seems to be an expert on such—ah— "literature." I have every confidence, however, that ARES will be adopted.

Ares—I'll call it that from now on—Ares is not like the real or the fictional Mars in one respect. It is a ringed planet. The ring is not as bright or obvious as Saturn's, but it's there all right—we saw it as a beautiful dim disc as we approached. As in the case of Saturn, most of it is contained within the Roche limit, and must be the remains of a small satellite which was drawn in and disintegrated. We are sailing in the midst of the ring now. This is not dangerous, no matter how it sounds, since we have matched speed with the little fragments in orbit near us. We occasionally have a small collision, but the ring rocks are small, and they clunk off our hull at speeds of only a few meters a second, so they're not worth dodging.

Ares has one moon, asteroid-sized, 50,000 kilometers out. If there were originally two, the resemblance to Mars would be that much closer.

But Ares is bigger than Mars, with a mass of .40 of Earth, radius .78, surface gravity .66g, estimated surface air pressure 800 millibars, 20 per cent oxygen. The day is 24.5 hours, and the axial inclination 20.2 degrees. All in all, it must be quite livable for humans—at the equator hot by day, cold by night, very dry. A climate like Egypt on the Nile—with the canals standing in for the old river. It's not perfect, of course; we could have done with more water; but it definitely falls within our definitions of "human habitable."

A pity that there is certain to be a native problem. We are sure that they don't have space travel—if they did they would certainly have visited their moon, which is a very easy hop up from their surface—but we've scanned that moon very thoroughly, total coverage, high magnification, and there's nothing. Not even a footprint. And yet there must be an old civilization down there—those canals would have taken thousands of years to build, at the very least.

Probably it's a tradition-bound society, like that of ancient China. So long as we take reasonable precautions, we should have no serious trouble with them . . .

III — The Chronicler

Summary of the Year 9-9-2-0-8-4, by Aoak, Scribe and Elder of Khadan

Nothing worthy of note for the first two-thirds of the year, and some members of the Order were beginning to wonder if Ayun's prophecy would be fulfilled. That elder, in official trance on last year-day, had pronounced with extreme emotion: "8-4, 8-4, and the stars will fall! Xuma, beware!" The last third of this year seems to have vindicated Ayun.

In the ninth month, a new Whirling Star appeared as if from nowhere and took up an orbit in the Ring-belt, where it still spins. And since then there have been curious happenings at various places on Xuma, some of them such that they could well be described as the fall of stars—at least, of little ones.

The very first of such incidents took place at Xarth, two days after the first appearance of Vepan, "The Young Object." We have an excellent account of this from one of our members who was there at the time. That one was attending the court of Retumon, Emperor of Xarth, whom we have been watching with interest for several years now, as he is an invert male of fierce personality and unusual ambition.

Retumon was holding court in the Throne Room of Xarth, listening to reports from his frontiers with Tlanash and Yelsai. He seemed particularly interested in the state of Yelsai's defenses, and was pleased at the weaknesses reported by his female general Yalxa. He had just declared his satisfaction, and promised that as a reward for faithful service Yalxa would share his bed that night, when there was an indescribable noise from the street outside—then a short silence, followed by screams. Our envoy, who was standing unobtrusively far back in the hall, near one of the windows, had also noticed a flash of light—very white light. The envoy was swiftly at the nearest window, and looking down could see bodies lying prostrate in that main street of the Palace Quarter.

Retumon had witnesses summoned at once, but not much could be got out of them. Clearly there had been some sort of explosion a few fathoms above the street level. No one was actually killed, though some suffered badly from shock and one female lost the sight of an eye. One witness reported that a small object like a stone about the size of a person's hand had been dropping from the sky just before the incident, and vanished in the explosion; but this was not credited at first, since the witness in question was a child of twelve years.

Later on, we came to believe that the child had reported faithfully what it saw. For it happened that over the next month there were many similar incidents, some in other cities, some along country canals, one even at a dam here in Khadan—and several times people noticed a falling stone just before the explosion. In one incident—this was in the main square of Kvaryla—the stone actually hit the ground and burst at once into countless fragments. The explosion was much less violent this time, and there was no flash of white light; on the other hand, one person was killed by a flying fragment, and many more were injured.

The fragments of this "stone" proved to consist of metal and some unidentifiable substances, and there were hints of intricate structure. One piece was transparent like glass, and curved like a fragment of a lens. We took this to our sensitive Ayun for psychometry, and when in deep trance Ayun murmured "The Eye of God." So after that, people nicknamed the falling stones "the Eyes."

Early in Tenth Month, the rain of Eyes ceased. Since then, there have been no dramatic developments in the Falling Stones mystery, but one—or perhaps two—strange stories have reached us from the territory of Yelsai. Both come from the same area, the West Canal not far from the Xarth frontier.

On Tenth Month, Day Twelve, just before sunset, the farmer Xyl was walking through her fields at Mile 2-2-8 when she saw a small object come sailing through the air from the northwest. By this time the news of the Falling Stones had reached even this country district, so Xyl threw herself flat on the ground and waited for the explosion. But there was no explosion.

After a while, Xyl got to her feet and cautiously went forward to the spot where the object should have landed. And she found it. It was no little stone, but a metal thing about half a fathom high, shaped a little like a hutch for yevets or poultry. It stood up on three small metal legs, and there was an open doorway and a sort of metal drawbridge leading from the ground into the dark interior.

Xyl did not like the look of the thing at all. It reminded her of the traps that she herself had set to catch wild sukins on the edge of the desert. And, as she watched, it functioned just like a trap. The place where the thing had come down was a patch of bare soil surrounded by reeds. Suddenly, a hamlor bolted out of this cover. Hamlors are inquisitive little animals, and this

14

one was intrigued by the strange metal object. It hesitated for a moment, then walked up the metal drawbridge. At the very top it paused, uncertain whether to go in or not.

But at once it lost the power of choice, for the drawbridge snapped up, bundling the hamlor inside, and sealing the metal trap completely. Xyl retreated at once, and it was well that she did so, for a few moments later there was a flash of light and a rumbling sound, and the metal trap rose into the sky on a column of flame. As Xyl watched, it disappeared high in the darkening sky, eastwards.

When Xyl told this story, her mayoress did not believe her. But we are inclined to think that her tale is true, for seven days later, on Tenth Month, Day Nineteen, a child disappeared from a farm at Mile 2-3-6 on the Yelsai West Canal. It was a well-grown child named Saimo, over seventeen years of age; its parents said afterwards that it had always been very inquisitive. Well, the evening that Saimo disappeared, a neighboring farmer reported that she had seen "a huge black thing shooting up into the sky, with fire coming out from under it." From her description, this flying thing was shaped like the one Xyl saw, but was two or three times as large.

The child Saimo has not been seen again. And one of the fields of Mile 2-3-6 was badly scorched by some unknown agency. Could it be that the child walked into a flying trap—a trap designed not for hamlors, but for persons?

If so, what is it that is haunting Xuma?

Every evening now we watch for the appearance of the new star Vepan, as it briefly skims our northern horizon. But it behaves now like any other orderly Whirler of the Belt, and gives no sign.

What will the year '0-8-5 bring? Ayun was in trance today. The prophet mumbled two sayings: "The gods are white," and "Midwinter—death!"

We do not understand.

IV — The Zoologist

I don't know what day it is, and our new planetary reckoning has abolished months; I guess I could check, but what the hell, time is utterly weird on this voyage anyway. Unreal. When we left the Solar System I was 26—now what am I? By home reckoning, it is 24 years later, so I should be 50! An elderly woman. If I had left parents alive when we blasted out, they would be dead now—certainly dead before any message could link us across that terrible emptiness. But no one in this ship left parents alive—we were selected to avoid that, for the sake of emotional stability. Parents had to be dead, preferably from unnatural causes so as not to reflect on our own viability. Well, there were plenty of unnatural causes available in the System: pressure-dome accidents, visits to Earth . . . I don't know that the results have justified the theory: Dave Weiser, our top psych man, has had to work all out to keep us sane, and *he* has to keep sane by taking long hours off on his hobby, which is ponic farming.

Where was I? When was I? How old am I?—Hey, for that matter, who am I? I'd better label this tape: this is Sally Freeston's diary, which I haven't kept up properly since we got into orbit round Ares—I've been busy working on our zoo specimens. Anyway, this is the first entry since we switched to planetary reckoning.

I feel a bit like a zoo specimen myself. What with relativity effects and 8 years on ice, my physical age is 28 plus. Plus a lot, I'd say! This has been quite a hellish voyage—bad enough in the nature of things, and some of my fellow crew-members don't make me feel any too cheerful. There are quite a few plain military men—they're supposed to be qualified engineers of various sorts, but many are qualified only in servicing and using lasers. Space marines. And the girls—we are mostly young and therefore lack clout. *I* am the most senior, think of that! The sexes are matched evenly in *numbers*, 50 of each, but the men hold the real power.

16

All very natural, since the real career of most of the girls will be to have children. We've got to *breed* our reinforcements.

I've often thought I should not have come. Why did I volunteer? Why did any of us? I suppose it was the hope of a new and more *natural* life. The super-scopes of Farside had shown us there was an Earth-type planet here, but we didn't expect intelligent inhabitants. We hoped for a new clean innocent world—instead we've found an old world with an ancient civilization, and if they're innocent we're not, and neither are our plans. I knew I'd be a colonist; I didn't realize I'd have to be an imperialist too.

I've only recently begun to feel better about things, because I've made some good friends and have something to *do* at last. The good friends are Rosa Meyer our botanist, and her friend Dave Weiser, and Jack Willis—one of the more intelligent engineers—and his girl Sheila who is a ponicist; and Tom Carson. I could go on for a long time about Tom Carson —I'll try not to. Tom is 30 in physical-equivalent time, brown-haired, grey-eyed, 175 centimeters tall. He puts on a regular-space-pilot-and-no-damn-nonsense act which I think is partly self-deception, partly protective coloration against the marines. He sometimes pretends the only literature he reads outside his specialty is vintage SF: I don't believe him. He did go out to Mars when young as an ordinary astro man, but then he remembered that there was such a thing as culture in the System, and took a linguist's degree at Plato. Russian and Chinese, of course, but also some extinct languages, and Earth history. He came into Operation Breakout, he says, because otherwise he'd surely have been pressured into the spooks' brigade, and he didn't fancy that kind of life, hanging round the embassies and delegations in Tycho, and listening in via the latest bugs to Chinks and Russkies making love . . .

And now, Tom has hit the jackpot. It is 30 days since we scooped up that poor little Artian, and Tom is learning the first *new* language to be discovered in a century, the first *extra-terrestrial* language ever. I am, too, a bit, because I am helping Tom—quite officially, since I examine the little native as a specimen of animal life and look after his or its physical welfare. Poor thing, he was terrified when we first got him. That's easy to understand. How would *we* feel if we walked into a thing like a small metal hut, and then the door slammed on us and we were whisked up through hours of darkness into a ship full of alien monsters? Our little victim was in shock at first, and it took all Dave and I and Tom could do to bring him round.

Tom did the most, really: he spent hours of his time with the native, and finally took to sleeping in his cage. Yes, cage! We hope to convince the powers-that-be soon, to let the little fellow out of there. He is certainly not in any sense dangerous, and he deserves to be treated like a human being. He has developed a sort of anxious crush on Tom—Dave says it's a "transference," and proves that Artian psychology is very like ours. The native doesn't like to be separated from Tom for a moment. This may be touching, but frankly, it's messing up an important area of my social life . . .

The little native is very humanoid—we had guessed he would be from the probe photos, but it's even more startling than we thought. Our Artian has red-brown skin, and black hair only on the head and in eyebrows, almost exactly like us. Slanting, golden-irised eyes; snub nose; largish elliptical ears; four toes; six fingers. Comparison with other native animals shows that six was the primitive number of digits on feet too: the Artians must have lost two toes, which shows they've been ground bipeds much longer than we. But this is a minor point.

There is really only one striking difference, but that really *is* striking—*there are no obvious sexual organs whatever!* Between the legs, in front, he she or it has no pubic hair and no orifice or projection—the whole area is as smooth as a child's armpit. He—let me call him "he" for convenience—he has one outlet behind for solid and liquid excretion; possibly his sex works through there, too, but from the X-rays I don't think so. The non-rational creatures we've scooped from various sites don't help to solve the mystery, they only broaden it. Most of them have male or female sex or-

gans between the rear legs, and the system is quite separate from the excretory one; but three small mammals
are like our native, sexless.

I am not even sure our native should be called a
"mammal." He is warm-blooded, but there is no trace
of breasts or even nipples. No navel, either—a real
smooth customer! I wish we could ask him himself
about these matters, but we haven't got enough vocabulary yet. The creature calls himself Saimo—no, the
vowel's a bit longer, Sah-ee-mo . . . but whether that's
an individual name or the name of the species we still
don't know. He also sometimes calls himself *vep*.

Here's the latest news flash: those noises on the tape
were Tom coming in. He thinks he's solved "vep." He
gave Saimo an illustrated book showing humans at
home in Lunaris—men, women, *and children*. Saimo
uttered a cry, pointed to the kids, and said "Vep!"
Then he pointed to himself, and repeated it. So, he's an
Artian *kid*. We don't know how old, but on the evidence of relative size, I'd say a teen-ager, or the local
equivalent. So we've done a bit of child-snatching. How
nice.

Tom says he hopes for a real breakthrough on the
language pretty soon. I sincerely hope so. For one
thing, we need the language before we can contact the
planet, and brother, do we want to contact that planet! I
am fed up to my pretty back teeth with this flying
squirrel cage, and so are most of us.

For another thing, I hope Tom will be able to ease
off his work on Saimo when he has gotten his breakthrough. I really would like to see more of *him*. Just
now he rushed out to get back to work, and he didn't
even kiss me . . .

V — The Captain

Captain Mannheim, in starship *Riverhorse I*, in orbit
around Ares, 7/1/2143 home reckoning. Actually, for
routine purposes we are now keeping neither home nor

voyage reckoning—we are on Artian Prime Meridian Time. We adopted the northern winter solstice as New Year's, and the Artian year of our arrival as Year Zero. We arrived near the end of Year Zero, so we are now in Year One, Day 73, just past the northern spring equinox, since there are 288 days in the year—local days, that is. There's been no trouble about the longer day—everyone's circadian rhythms have adjusted fine to the 24½-hour cycle, which we call 24 new hours by making our clocks run slow. Thomas Carson, who had a spell of duty on Old Mars before joining us—well, he says our new time feels quite like old times. Sorry, future listeners—that's the sort of feeble witticism our great linguist goes in for.

This record will be largely concerned with Carson, I guess. Ever since he was dehibernated I've been a bit perturbed about him—he seemed both unsettled and unsettling. I had the psych team give him a thorough check, but there was nothing in their report to justify refreeze or even off-duty relegation. Dr. Weiser wrote (and I quote his dictoscript): "A tendency to satire, even to cynicism is not necessarily a maladjustment to the situation in which we find ourselves." Uh, I guess Weiser is alluding to the lonesomeness of this place— 20 light years out and no chance of conversation with the folks back home or elsewhere. There's no message yet from the other Operation Breakout ships, barring that brief one from Epsilon Eridani, where it seems they're trying to colonize a lunar-sized airless planet; we can't expect to hear from the Delta Pavonis ship for 18 years. For all we know, we may have found the *only* habitable planet in Near Space.

Carson made a crack about that early on: "The trouble with habitable planets is, they are likely to be inhabited by other guys." Those other guys are our problem now. In the—uh—critical situation of the human race back in the home system, and the possibility that there is simply no other habitable planet within feasible distance, we have surely *got* to persuade the Artians to make room for us in their world. And to do that without inflicting unnecessary damage on the local ecology, we've got to contact the Artians in the verbal

20

mode. And here, I must say, Carson, in spite of his abrasive manner, has been doing a pretty good job with the informant available to us, an immature native whose name is something like "Simon."

The language, apparently, is comparable to Chinese in that there are phonemic tones—but only two, and hardly anything in the way of inflections. It's not nearly as difficult sound-wise as we had feared, since the Artian speech organs are remarkably similar to the human ones. But in conquering the language we are up against a semantic block. At present Simon is learning *our* language faster than Carson is learning his. This is not because Carson is dumb—far from it, he's achieved miracles in sixty days of intensive work, and nobody else among our crew can match his facility. But the thing that keeps bugging us is that we don't have the referents at hand for the new words Simon keeps giving Carson. The photographs taken by our unmanned probes near ground level helped a bit, but after we got "street" and "canal" and "person," and so on, we were stuck. I suppose we could wait till Simon has learned English thoroughly, and then conduct a dialogue with him, but none of us wants to wait that long. Least of all Carson.

He wants to go down there.

We have discussed the question at length in formal Ship's Council. I too was in favor of a landing, but a landing in force. Carson swung the vote against me. Well, I guess I have to accept that, since by the ship's constitution in non-emergency situations I am only a constitutional monarch. Carson's argument was eco-political—if we landed in force we would bring out the Artians in battle array against us, and we'd be forced to slaughter them in droves. I myself can't see that a little show of force at the start would do any real harm. They will have to learn that their swords and spears mean nothing against our lasers. Carson says he can achieve the same effect single-handedly, and without loss of intelligent life. Yes, single-handedly: he has got a mandate from the Council to go down *alone*. Correction: with no other crew-member; he is going to take

21

Simon back with him, partly as an interpreter, partly as a gesture of good will.

"We gotta get the kid home," Carson said. "After a couple of months, his mom will be getting worried."

I call this pussy-footing. Carson is taking quite a risk going down like this, and I wish I could make the others see it my way. Luckily, we have agreed on measures which will safeguard *us* if things go wrong. There will be a combination lock on the lander door, with a backup self-destruct mechanism against forcible entry, so if Carson is killed or captured the natives won't get their hands on anything useful to them. In that case, we will be minus one small astroplane lander and one brilliant linguist, but I guess we'll have enough of the local language to communicate our intentions so long as they are emphasized by *other measures*.

The basic plan, of course, is 2/3/A—for use on intelligent but technologically backward and politically disunited species. It is a method which has proved its worth time and again in Earth history. It does not necessarily involve large-scale devastation or population crash. In the worst cases on Earth, the real villains were not the conquerors but the bugs they brought with them. Well, we've made thorough tests on Simon, and luckily the species are too different genetically to pose any mutual threat through the parasites of either—though, again luckily, they are similar enough in basic chemistry to eat and enjoy the same foods.

The Artians will survive—so long as they see reason, and play ball with us.

Carson will be leaving within 48 hours. I hope he will make adequate recordings of what he finds—he sometimes shows a bad tendency to keep his thoughts to himself . . .

PART ONE

The Coming of
the Gods

Chapter One

When I took my finger off the burn-button, and we began our de-orbit drop towards the planet we had nicknamed "Ares," I wished for the nth time that that old SF device had really been feasible—an instant universal translating machine. But there is no such thing, and can't be. So, still lacking just the right words for a tense situation, all I could do was look at Saimo strapped down beside me—and smile.

Saimo smiled back. The facial gesture seemed to mean the same for that kid as for me; but I still wasn't absolutely sure. There was a hell of a lot I wasn't sure about regarding that kid.

Mind you, we'd come a long way in the past twenty or thirty days. We'd established that (1) the native name for the planet was "Xuma" (2) there were many nation-states on it (3) but only one language and one intelligent race. Saimo's nation was a city plus adjoining segments of canals, the city lying at about 20 South Latitude, 30 West, and in Xuman named Yelsai.

We still hadn't established which sex Saimo belonged to. The little Xuman animals we'd scooped up seemed to belong to *three* sexes, males, females and neuters.

Most of the neuters were young ones, but there was one neuter rodent which was definitely *aged*. Female mammals had nipples, males and neuters had none. Questioning Saimo directly didn't help all that much—on one occasion he seemed to say there were *four* sexes! For one thing, he was badly confused about *our* sexes, at least to start with. When I took off my shirt, that first time in his cell, I'll swear the kid looked at my nipples, and classified me as a motherly type! We got that cleared up later, but Sally Freeston and I both had to strip down in the interests of science to do it . . .

Saimo himself, when naked, was a strange sight, beautiful but disturbing. Sally had taken to calling him "the Angel." Well, that was suitable in many ways. He had a sweet temper. He was 160 centimeters tall, i.e. grown-girl-sized. Fine smooth red skin, lovely golden slanted eyes, cute nose, black hair. At a *very* casual glance, he might almost have passed for a sunburnt Chinese girl or teen-age boy. I know there were all sorts of minor things and that one major thing unhuman about his structure, but superficially . . . well, his curves were girlish, and he had a very human backside . . .

Saimo was not shy about his body. When he was captured by that flying rat-trap, he had been naked. Since then, the powers-that-were had given him a pair of shorts—for reasons which I sometimes discussed with Dave Weiser! I guess he brought out the latent homosexuality in some of us.

And now, here was Saimo, tucked into a girl's pressure-suit and strapped to the seat beside mine, as we dropped past Xuma's ring on the south side, heading for *Yelsai xir xul da-iid-sai*. That was Saimo's home address: Yelsai Canal West 2-3-6.

As one might have guessed from the number of fingers—six—the Xumans counted by dozens, so "2-3-6" actually meant "288 plus 36 plus 6," i.e. 330. Saimo's *thon* (farm? village?) lay 330 *idaz* north of the city of Yelsai on the canal next to the Western (dry) Ocean; and an *idaz* was damn near an old Earthly mile—actually, 3 times 1728 Xuman feet. I'm glad Saimo was a whiz-kid at math—we had now got the number-system and the measures just fine. The basic measure of length for the Xumans was the *thap*, which meant "foot," the part of the body, and Saimo's foot measured 27 centimeters from heel to first toe, nearly as much as mine. The Xumans never had any problem of decimalization—everything was base 12 to start with. Just like us, they had 24 hours in a day, and 12 main divisions in the year; unlike us, they had 24 days in their "months," and a perfectly regular calendar. Twelve is a much handier number than ten, of course, and they used natural body measures of length, not abstractions like our "meter." As somebody once said, in some solar system or other, the (Xu)man is the measure of all things.

And yet, having got that far, all that I could do now to reassure Saimo was to smile.

He smiled back, and moved his hand in its special mitten till his little sixth finger touched my glove.

"You here, Tomáss, I not afraid," he said. When Saimo spoke English, the effect was strangely beautiful: each syllable was clear and bell-like, mezzo-soprano, with accents marked by pitch, not stress. That's how you have to speak Xuman, of course—you half sing it.

As the astroplane dropped, I got Saimo to give me another singing lesson. I had just mastered the tone difference betmeen *xúl* ("west") and *xùl* ("excrete"), when we hit the atmosphere.

Our flaming missile stopped being a flaming missile, and automatically the wings flicked out. We began our glide-path over the Western Ocean, Laral Xul, which is a bleached dust bowl of salt deposits and bones of stranded former sea-creatures. Then we were over red desert, coming down low. Ahead of us suddenly was the blue-green streak of the canal.

Saimo said nervously, in English: "Rai', rai', Tomass! If you go lef', you hit Ksarth. Ksarth no good! Bad persons!"

"Another city?" I asked.

Saimo shook his head in the gesture which I knew meant "yes."

I had aero control now, of course, so I did a half-right turn, and filed the information: North of Yelsai is the state of Xarth, an enemy of Yelsai.

The blue-green canal area was now a broad patch ahead and to the left of us. Just before it there were pale projections rising from the desert like a row of teeth. I headed down towards them. As I got close, I could see that they were artificial squared-off slabs of stone sticking straight up like office-blocks in Plato or Lunaris.

"Nei tyaa?" I asked, pointing. "What are those?"

"Hudaan," said Saimo, looking frightened. That did not help: *hudaan* was a new word. (But *hud* meant "dead." So . . .?)

The desert on the west side of the *hudaan* was nice and flat, so I brought our little plane down there. I was glad I had had aero practice on Mars; only three other guys in *Riverhorse* had that, and the simulators aren't quite the same as open planet. Of course the air was thick here, much thicker than on Mars, nearly up to Earth standard; I wished briefly that I had had Earth flying experience—but of course, if I had had *that,* I would never have passed the medical for Breakout, only desperate characters visited that old slag heap these days. Anyhow, experienced or not, I made it down through those 800 millibars, and we hovered and came down gently in vertical mode.

Even before I had unstrapped myself, I felt the full horror of that enormous gravity.

Into the plane's radio I said: "The *Courier* has landed. And I guess I weigh a ton."

I weighed a ton because everything is relative. The *Riverhorse* living quarters, near the ship's outer hull, got the benefit of the maximum spin—which gave them Lunar-normal gravity. On Old Mars I had had to get used to twice that; but here on this New Mars the grav was *four times* that of my home planet. Of course, I had been practicing in the ship's centrifuge, but that was only for 15-minute periods. Now I had to stand up and walk under .66g for as long as I stayed on Xuma! The academic fact that I was an *Earth*-man (ha ha!) did not help a bit. (For that matter, I often wondered how our ancestors ever stood up on their native world.)

Saimo had unstrapped himself, and stood up, light and agile even in his pressure suit.

"We *home* now," he said. "Oh how good!"

I half rose from my seat, groaned, and slumped back. Getting up could wait. We knew the Xuman atmosphere was O.K. for human breathing, so now I pressed the vent button on my seat arm, and the air came whooshing into the cabin.

It was hot. Where we had landed, it was afternoon in a tropical desert.

"Wow!" I said. "We'd better get out of *these*." Saimo was already stripping off his pressure suit.

Gingerly I got up, taking care to keep my center of mass over the base formed by my two boots. I was starting to sweat. Out of the windows, the red desert looked like a shimmering furnace; inside the cabin, the ship's radio was filling the air with noise pollution.

"*Courier*, this is *Riverhorse*. Come in, please! Report current activities—"

"Okay, okay," I said. "Currently, I am undressing. Can't a man have any privacy at intimate moments?"

Saimo, now stripped to his bare skin, put out his slim six-fingered hands and caught me as I was about to fall over. Then he began helping me climb out of the suit.

So, I thought, this is the planet I suggested calling Barsoom. Hah! Canals and red-skinned natives, okay, but the gravity! Of course, you have to have high gravity if you want to breathe natural air. But I ain't going to amaze the locals with my super-Xuman muscles, my outstanding ability for jumping over their buildings . . .

Reality is never as satisfying as fiction. For another thing, as a means of transport the astral plane beats the astroplane hands down: John Carter never landed on Barsoom with Mission Control breathing down his neck. But that's just what Tom Carson *did*.

I got out of that elephantine suit at last, and stood up carefully in my black Breakout uniform. Then I put on the portable radio, which sat like a bulky collar round my neck and reared its aerial behind my head. I tested it, and it worked: worse luck.

". . . report current activities! . . ." I recognized the

voice of Bert Belmondo, the First Officer. B.B. was one of Mannheim's stooges, a real pain in the neck.

"Current activities nominal," I said. "Pressure equalized to exterior. Am about to open the door. Quit fussing, will you? The monitor in this gadget will tell you if I'm eaten by a wild zitidar."

"Last word not clear, Carson. Repeat. Do you detect dangerous fauna?"

"No, nothing, that was just a joke . . ." I reached for a certain tiny dial at my throat, and twisted it, and the static-toned voice quieted considerably. By rights, there should have been no such dial on my collar, but Jack Willis, my engineer friend, had fixed it on unobtrusively, according to my specifications, just before we pushed off. Now Big Brother in the sky would think my radio was acting up, but my heartbeat would come through nice and regular—I hoped. I didn't feel like making off-world conversation right now; there was damn-all that B.B.'s yattering on my chest could do to help me, and it could certainly hinder by distracting me.

We got the door open, and I strapped on my laser, shouldered my small pack of supplies, and waved Saimo out first. He jumped down easily, landing lightly on the red soil, and then I followed, lowering myself gingerly backwards down the short ladder, and locking the door as I went down.

My boots touched the surface, and I straightened. I let go of the ladder, and thought of making some historic statement into my throat mike— "one little step for a man," or something like that.

It's lucky my fingers hadn't actually reached that volume control when I uttered my first word—because by then I had lost my balance, and my first word on Xuma was actually "Fffuckkk!"

Saimo picked me up. "You are all right, Tomass?" he inquired anxiously.

"Sure," I said, "I just made a giant leap for mankind, that's all."

I had to lean on Saimo for a while before I could safely stand, and I had to hold his hand tightly as I learnt to walk. The heat did not help: it must have been nearly 35° C.

After about ten minutes I felt steadier on my legs, and was able to face the situation more calmly. I spoke a brief message into my chest radio—enough, I hoped, to keep my Collar-bone Critic happy—and then I and my Man (?) Friday set off on our stroll to the blue-green pastures.

The small orange sun was behind us as we stepped out from the long shadow of the lander. On three sides of us stretched the red desert, a flat sandy plain partly covered by drab yellow vegetation of various types, some mere ground weeds, others meter-high succulent plants that reminded me of cacti. I later learned that Saimo's people called this Western Desert the Desert of Death, but they have curiously positive ideas about death, and actually this red plain was very much alive in its own way. It was, literally, crawling—with invertebrate creatures like big crabs or scorpions, and dragon-like reptiles a meter or two long. All these beasts were reddish, and not easy to see unless they moved, and even then it looked as though the ground itself was moving rather than the animal upon it. That was what made most of the shimmer, in fact, not the heat haze.

I fingered my laser as a dragon scuttled past. He was all spikes and crests, and he stuck out a red tongue and hissed at us; but Saimo said he was harmless.

"He eat plants. Is afraid of us," he said.

Also, I must add, these dragons had only four legs—like all the other vertebrates of Xuma. The evolution of animals on this planet was very similar to that on Earth: unlike Barsoom, there were no six-limbed green "men," eight-legged "horses" or ten-legged "dogs." The fish that climbed out of Laral Xul, like any well-designed fish, had only four main fins, so the well-designed land animals were all tetrapods.

We plodded on. The sun blazed out of a cloudless deep blue sky—a sky of a darker blue than the old films show as the Earth sky-color. I guess that's because the sun of Xuma is smaller than Sol, and the air is a bit thinner than Earth's. The smallness of the sun gave a slightly sad effect to the light—as when at home Sol is in partial eclipse, or like the sunlight on Old Mars. But because this sun was more orange, the sadness was a warmer, richer sadness—a faded, mellow light.

And yet by contrast some things showed up brightly. So now, ahead of us, fully lit up by the rays of the sinking sun, lay the line of hudaan.

There were four of these slab-like monuments a couple of hundred meters east of us, with suggestions of others in similar groups to north and south. As we drew nearer, Saimo pressed my hand and suggested we move to the right and give them a wide berth. He said, in Xuman:

"It is not custom for me to see these things, because I am a young one."

I yielded, and followed him around. Saimo now was turning his eyes away from the hudaan, but there was no reason why I should; and immediately I saw what it was that might frighten him.

The slabs had a high ledge below their tops, and on the ledges gleamed long whitish things. More of these white things lay in crumpled heaps on the ground just before the hudaan; and suddenly I realized that they were bones. Skeletons of Xumans. Sally could have a field day here comparing the structures of the various sexes and ages . . . And in the air above the great slabs there were birds wheeling and soaring—Xuman vultures, or the equivalent.

I now asked Saimo a few questions. The poor kid obviously hated to linger here, but he humored me—and confirmed my suspicions. The Yelsaians did not bury or burn their dead—like the Parsis of ancient India, they exposed them as food for carrion-birds. The hudaan were the local equivalent of Towers of Silence.

"They line the west side of our canal," said Saimo, still keeping his eyes turned carefully away from them. "If you had landed on the east side, Tomáss, we need not have seen this fearfulness."

"Are Xumans so afraid of dead bodies?" I asked.

"Not males, females, or old ones. But we young ones must not see before our time."

Then we had passed the slab-tombs, and between

their huge shadows the blue-greenness of the canal lay before us.

The canal area was a valley running north and south in a slight depression several kilometers across. Abruptly, a few meters before and below our feet, the red dust and the ochre weeds gave place to tall bluish reeds, blue-green grass-like plants, and clumps of things like bulrushes or pampas grass. Beyond a short strip of this bush lay squares and more squares of fields; bluish, greenish or golden fields punctuated by tufts and lines of trees. The trees reminded me of those I had seen in Lunaris under the great dome of Tropical Park—palms and papaws and banana and bamboo. The trunks were mostly slim and spindly, soaring out into great green fans or feathery leaves ten and twenty meters above ground. The whole scene was surprisingly lush, in dramatic contrast to the desert plateau we were just leaving.

And there were buildings. The nearest, islanded in some fields only a couple of hundred meters away, was a low pavilion of yellowish stone with a flared roof of blue tiles; there were several similar ones scattered about the valley. In the distance, beyond these pavilions, I could make out a whole line of more elaborate buildings at what I guessed was the bank of the canal itself; and beyond that were more masses of trees, rising slightly towards the horizon.

For several seconds I stood as though petrified, paralyzed. I had never seen anything like this in my life— the living countryside of a living inhabited planet under its own natural sky. Poisoned, blasted Earth, where my father had died, was an impression only from books and films; and of course on the Moon life was a set of domed pimples and rock tunnels surrounded everywhere by lethal void. Even on Xuma, I realized, life had a hard struggle, but nothing to the struggle life had made for itself in the system of Sol.

Looking up at the gently waving fronds of the trees, and above them at the dark blue of the empty sky, I felt irrational panic. The city-dome had burst, was gone, and in seconds the blackness of space would come

rushing in, spilling the living breath out of the lungs of
the people . . .

Then Saimo, my naked red-skinned Angel, put his
six-fingered bare hand in mine, and smiled.

"Yelsai West Canal," he said. "Tomass, how good
that you bring me home. You are so good, Tomass, I
love you!"

I smiled too, awkwardly, and patted his shoulder. I
was well aware that Saimo had this desperate affection
for me. In *Riverhorse* we had terrified him, and then
more or less brainwashed him, one among many items
of our guilt, and now I had to make it up to him.

"Let's go," I said.

We strode through the strip of bush. Already I could
see people ahead—in the field before the yellow-walled
pavilion there were a half dozen red-skinned figures,
some naked, some apparently partly clothed.

The next moment, Saimo screamed.

I whirled, and saw what he was looking at. From our
left, from the huge jagged tooth-row of the hudaan,
there now poured into the valley a stream of—horse-
men. Well, cavalry. Some of our city-probes, in the seconds before they exploded, had shown such, but my
view of them now was much clearer.

The red-skinned warriors were wearing nothing much
more than short leather kilts, plus some straps to support their weapons, which were swords and lances. But
their heads were almost totally covered with mask-hel-
mets of silvery metal obviously designed to suggest
death's heads—the Xuman skull stripped of its flesh is
very humanoid, and I got the idea at once. These riders
were obviously out to inspire terror—and by god, they
were succeeding—even with me, I might say. But their
"horses" provided some comic relief—they were tall,
spindly-legged beasts with padded feet, long necks, and
absurd big heads, altogether like a mixture of the
earthly horse, giraffe and camel.

There were at least twenty riders in the first wave of
this horde, and they were bearing down very fast on the
country-folk by the pavilion, couching their lances and
uttering horrible yells.

"*Kunir xarth*," breathed Saimo, gripping my left

arm. "*Hudyo* . . ." I realized that he had said "Men of Xarth—killers."

The country folk had now seen the oncoming warriors, and were screaming and running for their lives. But they were obviously doomed, unless—

My right hand was already at my hip holster. I drew my laser, levelled it, and pressed the trigger.

A small tree beyond the field became timber. Then as the Xarthian cavalry reached that invisible line they began falling. First their mounts were cleanly beheaded, then the riders were cut in half at about waist level. In seconds, the whole of that first wave had become a butcher's shambles.

Behind them, other squadrons were cantering down into the plain—about a hundred mounted warriors. They whooped and waved their sabers—then when they caught sight of the carnage, they yelled with dismay, checked their animals, and milled about in a compact group. I thought I might as well make a clean job, I felt these guys would be no loss to the planet, so I thumbed my laser to full power, and swept it at them.

The whole troop disintegrated. One or two mounted figures darted back between the hudaan tomb-slabs, but not one of the warriors who had descended into the valley remained alive.

Then I clicked on the safety, and returned my laser to its holster. The whole "battle" had taken about three minutes. I suppose a real hero would have felt shame at butchering those noble savages like that with superior fire-power, instead of impressing them with his personal prowess. I felt no shame, only relief.

Saimo now threw himself on the ground, clasping my boots. His little red face was turned up to mine, and his golden eyes were gleaming. Xumans don't shed tears, but I guess if he had had tears, he would have shed them then.

"*Aanir inu,*" he was saying, over and over. *Inu* was "my," but *aanir* was a word I didn't know. I gathered, anyway, that he liked what I had done. But also, he was utterly awed. He had seen plenty of human "magic" in *Riverhorse*—but never a laser in action.

35

I turned up the volume on my radio.

"*Riverhorse*, this is Carson. The skipper should be pleased with me, B.B. I have just lasered about 100 hostile natives out of existence. They were enemy warriors about to massacre some local peasants. The peasants are now approaching me slowly—very slowly. Angel will explain to them that I'm on their side, and I expect friendly relations will now be established with the state of Yelsai, just as we planned. Over."

"Roger, Carson. That's fine. Look, we're about to go over the hill now with respect to you, will you please extend your Maxi aerial to maintain contact via relay satellite for the next few hours . . ."

The Maxi aerial was a metal foil like a fan about a meter across and high. With the damn thing extended, I would look like a marching tuba-player. Also, there was now a strongish east wind blowing, and with that surface up I'd be in real danger of being blown over.

"I fear my Maxi is jammed," I said. "If you don't hear a thing for two-three hours, please don't worry. The locals have arrived, and they're worshipping me . . ."

I turned down my throat dial.

The sun was now quite low on my back, and what with that strong breeze I was no longer hot—just pleasantly warm. Saimo was talking to the half dozen Xumans who had crept up to me, and I now got a good look at them.

Three were obviously *vep*, children—they were naked, and as sexless as Saimo. They varied in size, and in our terms they might have been about six, nine and twelve years old. I was intrigued to see that the smallest one showed traces of a rudimentary navel—the others did not. The other three Xumans were navel-less adults. Two, who wore short kilts of some woven material, I wanted to call men: they did not differ much in appearance from Saimo except that they were clothed where I would have liked to see them unclothed, and their voices were deeper than Saimo's. What made me especially sure that they were males was the appearance of the sixth Xuman. This one was clothed in a sort of green linen skirt from the waist down to about ankle-height, and her bare chest swelled at the right places into small conical breasts with *nipples*—which none of the others possessed.

"Kun?" I said, pointing to her. "Woman?"

Saimo shook his head sideways, which meant "yes." "She is the woman Lulen, a *psuyo*—that is, she works this land—and these are her two official men and their three children. The woman Lulen thanks you for saving the lives of her family. Now she invites you to come to the *thon* to be welcomed by the head woman. This *thon*, Tomáss—it is *da-iid-la*. 2-3-0. You landed so well, my *aanir*, we are only six miles from my home *thon!*"

"Saimo," I said, "what is *aanir?*"

He made a wriggling shrug of bafflement. "You come from the sky—you have such great power! There are tales among us of the *aan*, sky folk of great power. I think you must be that. *Aanir* is male *aan*. Just as *kunir* is male *kun*," he added, pointing to the two Xuman men.

So. I knew that in Xuman, *kun*, "woman," was the basic word, and the word for "man" was derived from that—just the opposite of English. Saimo had called me "my god"—or was it "my male goddess"?

By now more country folk had appeared and were flocking towards us, and I could see that they all fell into these three categories—naked sexless children, and kilted men, and skirted women with bare breasts and nipples. A few very small children had definite navels. All these people had red skins, black hair, and gold, gold-brown, or yellowish-green eyes; and I thought them all good looking, just as Saimo was good looking in his strange elfin way. The women wore their hair long, most commonly arranged in a single plait halfway down their bare red backs; the children and men wore theirs like Saimo, cut neatly above their shoulders. I noted that none of the children could be classified as boys or girls—or were they all boys? I asked Saimo, as best I could.

"No," he said, "not males, not females—they are *vep*. Like me."

"And when they are older," I said, "what will they become? Men or women?"

Saimo looked at me strangely, his cheeks turning a darker color, very much like a human blush.

"Men," he said. "At least—nearly always."

"Does something happen to their bodies—there?" I said, pointing to his groin.

"Yes," he said, blushing even more deeply. "The flesh opens." He gripped my hand. "Tomass—will you come now? The people will get you a—a *trolley*."

He used the English word for a piece of mobile furniture we used in *Riverhorse*. But in fact the vehicle of the Xumans wasn't a trolley—it was a light wooden cart or open carriage with four large slim wheels, and finely carved body-work painted in blue and gold. Saimo now explained that these were the Yelsai national colors, so the cart was state property. It stood on a neat roadway between two fields, and it was harnessed to one of those horse-giraffe-camels, whose proper Xuman name was *thapal* ("flatfoot").

The people helped me and Saimo up onto the cart, and a Xuman man jumped nimbly up to the driver's seat in front, jiggled the reins, and got our transport going. The thapal moved pretty much like a horse, except that it lifted its spindly legs very high. Soon we were making good speed in the direction of the canal; meanwhile, the crowd loped along the road after us.

We plunged into an avenue of trees with very regular fan-shaped leaves that met and interlaced overhead—they reminded me of banana trees except that their trunks were smooth brown tubes. A lot of Xuman trees and plants have this feature: they are efficient water-retainers. I turned to ask Saimo the name of the tree—and then I noticed that he was shivering and looking tense.

"What is it, Angel?" I said. "Are you cold now?" It certainly was cool in this avenue, but Xumans resist changes of temperature much better than we do, and I had not thought Saimo would need any covering yet. But now he nestled against me, putting his arm round my waist.

"Tomass," he said, "I—yes, I am a little cold." He lowered his voice. "Tomass, will you be good to me?"

"But Saimo, of course—"

"Not so loud then." He was whispering; then a thought struck him, and he switched into English. "Tomass, I—I have a little pain inside, between the legs. It is the first sign, I think."

"Of what?"

"Of my—change. They say fear will do it, and I am of the right age, and I have had much fear. Usually they take the *vep* of one-six years—I mean, of eighteen— they take them up to the hudaan and show them the dead bodies. The fear of death makes them become men."

"Are you becoming a man?" I said, grinning. "Congratulations!"

Saimo looked troubled, and grasped me even more tightly. "Tomass—if anything go wrong with me, will you help? Tell them you need me for talking to people—don't let them take me away!"

"My dear Angel," I said, putting my arm round his shoulders, "you can bet your last Euram dollar I *won't* let them take you away. Not even if you turn into a—a thapal. I shall use my privileges as a god. But say, what about your own family?"

"My mother is not far from here," said Saimo somberly, "but that one cannot do anything for me now. Since I was taken up, that one is become *uxan* . . ."

"Old?" I said. Saimo had uttered the word "uxan" when we had shown him pictures of grey-haired old human folk, but he had not been very certain about it.

"You will see," he said. "That one is in an uxan-house not far from here. It will come to see me, I think—maybe before anything happen to me."

"Saimo—are you in bad pain? Do you need help right away? We can stop the cart—"

"No. It don't happen so quick. But, Tomass—please ask them to let me sleep in a room alone with you tonight. And ask them for a Xuman man's clothing. I think my change will be finished in ten, twelve hours.

The first change is the swiftest—the others take many days."

"What other changes are there?" I said.

"The second change—for most people," said Saimo darkly, "is from man to woman. The third change is from woman to *uxan*. Now, do you understand?"

"O my god," I said—for I did understand. Our soft-lander scoops had picked up enough small Xuman creatures to suggest that there was something decidedly odd about the life-cycle of some of the planet's mammals. One little rabbity creature, which Saimo had called a *hamlor*, had changed sex from male to female during its last month in *Riverhorse*.

"My mother's former man," said Saimo, "my—stepfather?—he is now in the sick-house of our *thon*, he is in change to become a woman."

When I found my voice, I said: "How many years do you stay a man? And then, how many years a woman?"

"Normally," said Saimo, "the *vep* changes at one-six—I mean, eighteen years. Then for two-zero years—pardon me, Tomass, I cannot think in your numbers—for two-zero years, till the age of three-six, he is a man. Then for another two-zero years, she is a woman. After that, from five-six years, it is an *uxan*."

"The *uxan* has no sex?"

"No more than a vep," said Saimo. "The flesh heals smooth."

"Why don't we see any uxan in the fields?" I asked, looking round. "Or are there some?" From what I could see, there were only men, women and children about, and there were no signs of aging among the adults. But for what Saimo had just told me, I would have guessed that most of the men and women were about the same age—youngish.

"The uxan live a life apart," said Saimo. "You will see some at the canal, I think—many of them become canal workers. Others become teachers; and some go the long journey to the cold places."

"Eh?"

"To Khadan, at the end of the canals in the south. Or to the north ends, maybe, I think. I do not know this well—people do not talk about it to *vep*. I am sorry, Tomass, you must ask others. Oh!"

He gave a gasp. "What is it?" I said.

"The pains—they are getting stronger," he said. "I am glad that it is becoming dark. Soon I will begin to bleed . . ."

Chapter Two

We were approaching civilization. First, we came out onto a main north-south road, on the far side of which stood a line of yellow-walled, blue-roofed buildings. Beyond the buildings I caught a glimpse of water—the canal. The road was very smoothly paved with white stone blocks. On it was passing a sparse traffic of pedestrians, cart-travellers and an occasional thapal-rider—all red-skinned Xumans, men, women, and naked children. I got the impression of much variety of dress among the thapal-powered travellers.

"It is the big road between cities," explained Saimo. "In the early morning it is more crowded. Some of these folks are not of Yelsai—they will be going to the sleeping place set aside for them by the *thon*."

"Tell me more about this *thon*," I said.

It seemed the thons were village communes, spaced every two miles along the canal at the even-numbered milestones. The thon owned all the land on both sides of the canal and most of the buildings—the major exception being properties of the uxan (elders). The farming near the settlement was a collective affair, but outlying farms were leased to individual women. The head of the thon was a *kunal* (mayoress) elected by all the women of the thon.

"Don't the men have a vote?" I gasped.

"Oh no," said Saimo, "the women say that the men are too young. When they become women, then they can vote. Besides, the men are not always in the thon. For two years they have to leave and be soldiers—to serve the Queen."

"Queen? Oh yes, that figures," I said.

We were rattling on southward, and I was causing quite a stir among the other travellers, when at last we came to the main settlement. Here the buildings lining the canal were gapped by a broad bridge; beyond the bridgehead they rose again, now forming a single large block several stories high, composed pueblo-wise of adjoining units of different heights. There were several towers, some with flat roofs, some with flared roofs of blue tiles which looked nearly black in the last red rays of the setting sun. Directly opposite the main entrance of this block, on the other side of the road, stood a slim obelisk—the milestone 2-3-0.

Our driver turned in to the porch-like entrance, and a few moments later we were getting down amid a growing crowd of people. Some were dressed more elaborately than the average peasant: there were males in longer blue or white kilts and neck ornaments of what looked like gold, and females in long dresses with stiff high collars which still left their breasts proudly bare. I guessed at once that a civic reception would be laid on for us; but I was in no mood for this, and I knew it was the last thing Saimo needed.

"Tell them we're both tired," I said, "and ask for whatever medical supplies you need. I don't want to meet the Lady Mayoress and her gang right now. Get us a room somewhere, will you, Angel? Tomorrow morning will do for the take-me-to-your-leader stuff. O.K.?"

"Okay," said Saimo, with a brave smile, and began a long musical patter to the Xumans: *allegro con moto* con gestures. He pointed to the sky, and to me, and he used the words *aan* and *aanir* and *Xarth*. The locals were greatly impressed. After a while Saimo's solo became a duet with a fine-looking woman in a high-collared dress and a gold neck-chain. Finally she nodded, in that curious movement which looked like *no*, but meant *yes*.

Saimo turned to me. "Tlavei the Mayoress will give us a room in her own block, and everything we need, and leave us quiet till next sunrise."

"Good boy," I said, "let's go."

Tlavei led us into the building, and the crowd followed at a respectful distance. The place was a stairwell, softly lit by wall-globes which emitted a yellowish-white glow. I caught glimpses of frescoed walls, and a staircase which we now climbed. Luckily, I was growing used to the gravity . . . At last Tlavei threw open a door, and we were there.

She bowed deeply. "All you need we will bring," she said. "Rest well, good god, and little *vep*."

Our guest room was the most honorable in the mayoralty. It was on the top floor of a tower, and had windows on three sides, north, east and south. Each window was fitted with glass panels and wooden shutters, all of which could be slid in and out of the thick stone wall, moving easily on metal frames into precisely cut grooves. The evening was not yet cold, so I opened the east window and looked out.

In the violet sky the first stars were pricking out—but I had seen enough of stars lately; I was more interested in the view downwards. Directly below lay the canal. It was a waterway cut straight as a laser beam, with white stone banks and paths on either side—in this reach it was about 80 meters wide, with a long narrow stone island in the middle. To our left, a little way up, that bridge crossed the canal on two gracefully curved arches, with a pier on the central island.

There were connected buildings on the other side of the canal, and low ones even on the bridge—in fact, the main thon block seemed to be continuous from our side to the other side of the water. The general effect was like some medieval place on old Earth, a castle in sections spanning a moat, or maybe the lost city of Venice. But the style of the buildings was not much like

ancient Europe, it suggested partly old China, partly
the pueblos of the Amerinds. And partly it was like
nothing on Earth—the buildings soared to slim towers,
like our own Lunar housing, yet the soaring was done
not by concrete or metal or plastic, but by solid stone.
In the glow of the twilight stars, and the faint glimmer
of Xuma's ring, that towered village and canal looked
magically beautiful.

And old—you can't build like *that* in a hurry. I
turned to Saimo, and asked him how long the village
had been here.

"I do not know exactly," he said, "but all the thons
on this canal must be more than *kau thaz* years old . . ."

Kau thaz meant 12 to the fifth power—over 200,000
years! Yes, even allowing for the shorter year of Xuma

. . .

"The canal itself must be nearly as old as our time-
reckoning," added Saimo, "for all the main canals of
Middle Sector were laid out before the year *kau thaz*."

"I thought this was only your year 8-5," I said feebly.

"Yes, 0-8-5, Tomass. That is the short way of saying
it. In the full way, this is Year 9-9-2-0-8-5."

"More than *two million*," I gasped. "Two million
years since what?"

"Since the Order."

"What does that mean?"

"I am not sure. It is just what people say. I think the
Order means the Elders. I am very ignorant, Tomass."

There were two low beds, or rather mattresses covered with some kinds of cloth quilts arranged along one
wall of our room, and Saimo now sat down abruptly on
the edge of one of them. I guessed that he was in pain
once more, but there was nothing I could do. He had
already told me he would not need any kind of medical
help, just water to clean himself up. And we had that:
in one corner was a wash place, with a stone ewer and
basin and a hole in the floor to let waste water run
away.

Just then a musical voice outside the door said *"Pui"*
("here"), and in came Tlavei the Mayoress and four
well-grown children. The kids wore nothing but some

golden neck ornaments; I gathered that two were
Tlavei's own children, and two belonged to her sister.
They were just as excited and inquisitive as human children would have been to meet an extra-solar guest in
Lunaris; but Tlavei kept them on their best behavior,
and I'm afraid they found Saimo sadly uncommunica-
tive. In any case, they were here to serve us, not make
conversation. They brought in a low table and food and
drink to place upon it, and Tlavei presented Saimo with
a couple of linen kilts. Eying me shyly (or was it
slyly?), she murmured:

"If the god would care to wear one, I think he would
look very nice in it. It would be a pleasure for me to
present him with neck ornaments, too . . ."

"No, thank you, mayoress," I said in my best
Xuman. "I would feel cold. But thanks for your
kindness."

She gave me a curious, half-disappointed smile; and
then they all went out.

"Well," I said to Saimo, "here you are, Angel: now
you can clothe your nakedness."

He flushed. "I will not do that till my change is over.
It is not customary for *vep*. Tomass, I must tell you
one thing. When a Yelsai woman offers a man *neck ornaments*, it means . . ." He told me.

I whistled. "You don't say! Some lady, that mayoress! Have I offended her, then, turning down her ornaments?"

"Oh no. I do not think she seriously expected . . .
But women will always try, when they see a handsome
male. Shall we eat now, Tomass?"

Boy, I thought, is this a screwy planet! Not much
like old Barsoom after all! Here the *women* were the
wolves, and the poor little men had to watch out for
their virtue. I asked Saimo, and he confirmed my suspicion—yes, there were more men than women—there
had to be, because the death-rate eliminated some men
who therefore never became women. For which reason,
in Yelsai a woman was allowed two husbands.

We ate. I first hauled a little gadget out of my
pack—we called it a Taster—and fed samples of everything into that before I fed them into me. The Taster

gave the same verdict in every case: NONPOI-
SONOUS. I agreed with him. In fact, not only was the
food nonpoisonous, it was delicious—all the strange
vegetables, the Xuman bread, the small portions of
meat. I could forget about those tubes of emergency
pap in my baggage from now on. There was even a
sweetish cold yellow wine which would have made
connoisseurs in Lunaris rave.

I took a long cold delectable mouthful. "This is a
wonderful world you've got, Saimo," I began—and the
next moment there was a faint crackle from the region
of my collarbone. I looked at my watch: yes, *Riverhorse* was due round again. Cursing feebly, I turned up
the volume.

"Carson, come in, dammit; Mannheim here . . ."

"Okay, okay," I said, into my collar. "Carson here,
skipper. Program nominal as of now, all systems go and
lookin' good. Peaceful relations established . . ." And I
brought him abreast of events.

"So—you're resting up?" he said. "Are you reporting
excessive fatigue?"

"Well, plenty. This bloody gravity is quite a strain on
the feet, and I guess I walked half a kilometer this afternoon."

"Use native transport in future," snapped Mannheim.
"I take it you can command all the resources of the
state of Yelsai. Just one thing, make absolutely sure no
alien can get at your laser. You will sleep alone, of
course. You've enough equipment in your pack to rig
up a foolproof alarm. Got that?"

"Roger," I said, smiling across at Saimo. "I sure will
sleep alone tonight, skipper, even though the local gals
are shapely and willing."

"Look, Carson, cut out the wisecracks. You've done
all right so far, I suppose, but frankly I don't like your
attitude. Why the hell can't you keep in contact con-
stantly? Can't you fix that aerial?"

"No," I lied. "Don't worry, skipper, I'm in no danger
here. All the locals love me. Tomorrow we shall start
taking steps to see the Queen . . . oh, yeah, I should've
explained that, the head of state here is a female, like
the farmers and the mayors. But I guess, what with na-

tive transport, it may take me a day or two to meet her, and anyway I need that time to increase my mastery of the language and knowledge of local customs and so forth. Please, please don't worry. Look, can I speak to Sally Freeston? She's been studying the sex life of the native mammals, right?"

"Yes, but why—"

"It's about poor Angel. My indispensable interpreter seems to have reached the change of life—he's turning into a boy or something, and I do need expert advice . . ."

Mannheim spluttered. A few seconds later, I heard Sally's voice.

"Hi, Tom, how goes it?"

"Fine, Sal." I explained the situation.

Sally said, "Could you put Angel on the line? Yes, I said Angel. He's used to our communication systems. Get him to bend over your chest nice and close. We'll manage."

And they did. Apparently, Sally had made some kind of discovery in the last few hours, since I had left the starship. She began talking to Saimo, in a mixture of English and broken Xuman, about the sex organs of hamlors. I gathered she was asking him if the structures and changes were similar to those in Xuman *people*. Saimo said yes. And sukins? Yes, again.

"Well," said Sally, "looks like one in ten sukins goes through the changes the wrong way round, Angel. They turn girl first, then boy. At least, that's my theory. Does this happen with people? Over."

"*Kun* Sally . . ." began Saimo hesitantly, bending over my chest. *Kun* (woman) was a respectful form— almost a title. Saimo was silent for a second; then he whispered, "Yes, *kun* Sally."

"Okay," said the voice from my chest mike. "Angel, can you tell in advance?"

"*La*," he said. "No. Not till the change is beginning. People say—they say that *vep* who like finding out new things, those who play rough, run about much—they will be normal. I—I was very much one of that kind, *kun* Sally. That is why I was captured. But—they also say that *vep* who are much frightened before their right time, or *vep* who like very much some *man*—they may become—*kynthi*."

I broke in. "*Kynthi?* What the hell's that?"

Saimo said: "*Kun* is woman, *iti* is little, young. I—" He broke off.

Sally said: "What happens to a *vep* who goes *kynthi?*"

"They take her away," said Saimo, choking. "They say it is not a disgrace, only an accident, and she should be pleased to serve the state in the way she can. Maybe that is truly how people think in the city, in Yelsai. But it is not how we really think along the canal. Those *vep* from the country who go *kynthi*— they are taken to the city, or to the army, and they are trained to please men, because that is all they are good for, having neither the age of a woman nor the strength of a man. From this *thon*, a *kynthi* would go to the army, because the army is closer than the city. It does not happen very often here, only maybe one in two-zero times—one in twenty-four. But when it does, they take her away to the army pleasure houses."

"O my god," I said. At the same moment, Saimo sprang backwards away from me.

"I bleed," he said.

It was true. Between his legs there had now appeared a dark patch of raw flesh. He went and knelt in the wash place, and I knelt beside him with the ewer. Over the next hour we had the benefit of Sally's advice, as I described what was happening to Saimo. At the end of the hour, *Riverhorse* had passed beyond the eastern horizon, but there was no need for me to deploy the big aerial—we knew by now what the outcome would be.

The male organ of most Xuman mammals is shaped like a fin; in the intelligent species it protrudes about 6 cm. between the legs, like a lens seen edgewise. Oddly enough, the female organ also protrudes, but like a broad cylinder with a slot in its center.

By the end of that hour, Saimo's organ was definitely growing—and it was growing into the shape of a broad cylinder. With a slot.

He—I could not yet stop thinking "he"—was gulping rhythmically, in what I now knew was the Xuman equivalent of weeping. It was a small but heart-rending sound.

"Angel," I said, caressing his/her shoulder, "stop it, please. I *won't* let the army get you! Look, I don't think it's a disgrace—not a bit! Among us humans, young girls are quite a *normal* kind of creature. We *respect* them."

Saimo did stop gulping, and threw me a look almost of joy.

"Truly? It is so also in some cities of Xuma, I think. In West Sector, so travellers say . . . Anyway, if *you* are not ashamed, then I am not. O Tomass, my god, I love you—and that is why this has happened. Because I was so afraid, in the starship, and because you were so good to me, and I gave you my heart, and you are a male—therefore am I become *kynthi*."

My Angel then threw me a look almost of calculation.

"Perhaps—when this is finished," she said, "perhaps then I can please you—because you are not only a god, you are also a man."

"O my god!" I said.

"No, Tomass, you must not call *me* that. *You* are *my* god. I am only your little kynthi, your *thula*."

Dully, I called for another linguistic explanation. Soon I knew: *thula* meant "slave."

It was a harrowing night. Xuma is essentially a desert world, and like all deserts it has an enormous daily temperature range. By the time I had finished helping Angel to wash, I could have sworn the water in the ewer was on the point of freezing. My teeth were chattering, even though I had closed and shuttered all the windows. Saimo, still naked, did not seem to notice the cold.

"Let's go to bed," I said. "I'm sure you won't stain the sheets now." I had long since dumped my radio; now I stripped to my underwear, and dashed for the warmth of my bed.

But Angel was sitting *on* the other bed, looking at me as mournfully as a lost kitten.

"Please," she said. "Please, my master, I am so lonely." And she crept to my bedside.

"Oh, all right," I said. "But no funny tricks, mind! I only want to sleep."

"I too," said Saimo.

Moments later she was nestling in my arms, naked and warm under the quilts.

Chapter Three

People in novels often seem to wake up and not know where they are. I can't think why, if the surroundings are not misleading. Anyway, it's never happened to me. On this occasion, I had been dreaming that I was in bed with Sally—a very pleasant dream—when I surfaced out of sleep into shadowy daylight and found myself cuddling a red-skinned shoulder. Also, my body was being pressed down on that firm mattress with all the weight of infernal .66g. Instantly I knew where I was—on Xuma, and in bed with Saimo, my self-dedicated slave-girl and worshipper.

I froze. I mean that almost literally. It was frightfully cold, that early morning, and the coverings of that bed were designed for a hardy Xuman metabolism. I really should have worn my uniform to bed, or demanded twice as many quilts. I suppose the cold would have woken me sooner if the warmth of Saimo's body had not kept me half comfortable along one side. What to do now? If I got up to grab the quilts from the other bed, I would probably wake Saimo, and I didn't want that. Not yet—I wanted some peace, time to think. So I stayed where I was, huddling against Saimo for warmth. The kid sighed, stirred, then snuggled against me, but did not wake. Light was coming through the cracks in the shutters.

I tried to sort out my thoughts. I did not like them much. The only thing on the credit side was that Saimo and I had both gone to sleep quite promptly the night before. No complications there, yet—which was to the good, because I did not think my poor little mixed-up Angel was in a fit state, emotionally, to handle such. But, for the rest?

When I had first seen this planet big and clear on the scopes, I had jokingly suggested calling it Barsoom. Since then, in some ways, that had proved quite appropriate: canals, red men, even a few fierce warriors . . . And I was going to meet a queen—the queen of an ancient, beautiful, proud city. Perhaps I could fascinate her, sweep her off her feet, become a Xuman prince. Tom Carson, the Warlord of Yelsai . . .

Crap.

I wasn't cut out for that sort of act. I didn't feel in the slightest like a hero, and I wasn't one. I wasn't going to marry any red princess if I could avoid it— someone like Sally Freeston would suit me much better, physically and mentally. What was I, really? An invader— a bumbling invader, my whole heroism packed into my hip holster. My mission here was Plan 2/3/A—otherwise known as *divide and rule*. I was to impress the Queen of Yelsai with my gun, and offer her our services—the services of us sky gods—to conquer any national enemies she cared to nominate, such as (for a start) the people of Xarth. That would be only the start. We had chosen Yelsai as our base of operations on the basis of what Saimo had told us—Yelsai was quite a small power. (The invader should always side with the weak against the powerful—the pickings are better that way, and persuasion is easier.)

Once we had shown the Queen what we could do, we would offer her the empire of her whole world—literally—on condition that she make over to us a reasonable slice of it—the Ship's Council had suggested the lush-looking East Sector. What would happen to the people of the East, we hadn't quite decided yet. Probably some would be deported, but most could stay as our—well, servants. (The Xuman word would be *thula*.) We would try to treat our allies right, so long as they did not threaten our superiority—and how could they? It should all be a pushover. I had only to charm and impress the Queen in the same way I had charmed and impressed Saimo—a show of strength, coupled with a show of kindness . . .

Yes, I thought, and look at Saimo now, poor kid. Perverted. If we hadn't trapped him like a specimen, if I hadn't been "kind" when he was terrified, he would have grown up normal for his planet. A manly boy, and then a womanly woman at the right age. Now, what was he? A whimpering girleen, a thing the locals used only for prostitution. And that's just what we would be doing to Xuma in general—enslaving a two-million-year-old civilization, making a whole planet our prostitute.

I hated myself. And yet I couldn't go back on Plan 2/3/A. For one thing, the guys on the ship held the real power—laser cannon and a fleet of landers; if I double-crossed them, they would know what to do . . . For another thing—hell, we *did* need this planet. We had been two-plus years of living time out in deep space—twenty-four years of real time back in the System—and things were looking black on the Moon, what with the bad feeling between us and the Russ and the Chinks. Xuma might well be the last chance for the survival of *Homo sapiens*. And *Homo sapiens* included people like Sally Freeston and—Tom Carson.

There was no way out of the bind. All I could do was try to work Plan 2/3/A as humanely (and Xumanly) as possible.

Saimo opened her golden eyes. She smiled, stretched, and moved her mouth close to mine.

"I have seen, Tomass, in the ship. You gods touch lips, no? Will you—will you kiss me, please, my master?"

I kissed her. Xuman lips are small, firm, and very red. If I had not been musing guiltily just before, the touch of Saimo's little scarlet lips might have been intensely pleasant. As it was, it was pleasant enough to make me feel like a child molester.

The next moment a voice at the door said "Pui," and Tlavei the mayoress entered. (I may say that this was always happening in Yelsai: nobody ever knocked at a door, nor did they wait after saying "Pui.")

Tlavei looked surprised to see us still in bed, and perhaps more so to see us in the same bed. However, without comment she dumped on the floor a bundle she had been carrying, strode to the windows, and slid back the shutters. Bright yellow sunlight streamed into the room.

"I was cold—" I began to explain.

"Well," I have brought you a robe against the morning chill," she said briskly. "Now my children will bring food, and after that there are people you will want to meet." She went out.

Saimo sprang out of bed, and put on one of the men's kilts we had been given the previous day. It came down to a little below her knees. As I nerved myself to get out of the shelter of the bed-coverings, a thought struck me. Saimo's chest, in the golden sunlight, seemed to curve even more gracefully than yesterday.

"Are you going to develop *nipples*?" I asked.

She laughed. "Yes, master, but they may not come for some time—a few weeks. And even in normal boys the voice takes time to deepen. I can still pass for a young male for a while."

"It would be easier, if only you people dressed sensibly for the climate," I growled, leaping for my uniform. I whipped this on, then swathed myself in the new overgarment Tlavei had brought—a thing like a padded satin dressing gown. The Mayoress had also provided a short light cloak for Saimo, but Saimo ignored this, twirling round in her new kilt, apparently quite comfortable at being only *half* naked in that chill morning. It was no longer difficult for me to think of Saimo as a *she*—she was behaving like one, casting glances alternately at her curvy body and at me in a way which reminded me quite strongly of some *human* females I had known.

"Proper *Xuman* clothing!" she said, fingering her kilt. "Of course, it should be longer for a *kynthi*, but still

55

. . . I am no longer a naked *vep*! Do you like me so, Tomass? Am I *kela* (beautiful)?"

"Ravishing," I grunted, using the English word. I was not in the mood for this sort of conversation, for several reasons. For one thing, I was getting hungry; for another—

I asked Saimo a certain question.

"Oh," she said, "liquids here, in the wash-corner—you see there is a hole for them to run away. Solid you should void in a certain place at ground level. It is important not to waste any useful bodily substances. Even the waters that flow through that hole are used for irrigation."

"Well, I guess I gotta help the irrigation program," I said.

I was halfway through my irrigation project, and Saimo was watching with mild interest, when there entered, without even a "Pui," the Lady Mayoress and all her children, bringing breakfast.

The children nearly dropped the plates. I hurriedly turned away, and in a second or two got my pants zipped. Tlavei asked, with admiration:

"Do all gods have those excellent hose-pipes?"

"Only the males," I admitted.

Tlavei's golden eyes gleamed, and she began to question me as to the anatomy of goddesses.

"Saimo, you know—you explain," I said feebly.

Finally, we got breakfast: sweet Xuman pastry-bread, and a hot purple drink that was as stimulating as coffee and as richly satisfying as milk chocolate—Saimo called it *tlaok*, and said it came from a certain bean. In fact, the bulk of all Xuman food is vegetable-derived; the red folk do not keep animals for slaughter, and get meat only by hunting, mostly on the fringes of the deserts.

We were just finishing when I remembered my taskmasters on high. Hell, *Riverhorse* would be round again, and they wouldn't be getting even the monitor signal . . . I draped the radio round my neck, turned up the volume—and at once got Mannheim himself.

"About bloody time," he said, "I was just about to order down a search party. Carson, what the hell—"

"I gotta be comfortable," I said sulkily. "Ever tried sleeping in one of these outfits, skipper? Anyway, there's nothing more to report."

"Don't you dare take that radio off again—"

"Okay, okay," I said.

So all that day I went about with my massive collar-gadget on, and while I wore the over-robe the little antenna emerged from it and stuck up behind, a few centimeters behind my head. Maybe the natives thought this was some kind of godly neck ornament, smart wear for deities.

I also wore my laser in its holster, strapped over my robe, on my right hip.

At breakfast Saimo and I went out to meet the people. This occurred in a lower room of the thon block, where we found Tlavei and her two husbands—prettily dressed young men in blue kilts and gold necklaces—plus a number of (female) farmers—and two individuals of a kind I had not yet set eyes on.

Most of the locals were already undressed down to skirts—only for the warmth (!) of the morning, but these two wore long white sleeveless robes gathered at the waist by a yellow sash. Their exposed faces, arms and feet were a curious silvery grey color. Their features were perfectly Xuman, though more angular than those of children, males or females; and their hair was *yellow*, and closely cropped. I had seen blond hair a bit like that on many a smart young military officer in Lunaris—those of European or American Wasp descent; but on these grey-faced aliens the effect was bloody peculiar.

Tlavei bowed to me. "O god, may I present these *uxan* from the Gold-and-Silver Life-house—" she began.

But the next moment, Saimo uttered a cry, and flung herself into the arms of one of the grey-skinned elders.

"*Ma inu!*" she cried.

It is curious how constant one word is, even across twenty light years and several billion years of separate evolution: I suppose it is innate in mammalian sucking lips. As in so many Earth languages, *ma* in Xuman means "mother."

The elder touched Saimo briefly on the forehead, nuzzling with grey nose against red skin, and then pushed her gently away.

"Child," said the grey one, "you see that I can no longer be *ma* to you, since I am no longer woman. But it is good to see you in the world again, Saimo. So the sky gods were merciful! But what is the meaning of this dress you are wearing?"

"I have changed too, mother," said Saimo tremulously. "Now you must call me man, not child."

"Indeed?" said the other elder, with perhaps a touch of suspicion. "When were you taken to the hudaan?"

"Yesterday, by this god," said Saimo, indicating me. "The god wills that I be his interpreter now, he is keeping me by his side for this mission. He wishes to speak with the Queen in Yelsai—"

"We know that," said the elder quietly. "And so he shall. There will be time for that. First, we suggest that the god might like to visit our Gold-and-Silver House. After that, we can arrange transport to the city. Tell him."

Saimo explained. "The Gold-and-Silver House of Life is where the younger *uxan* preserve learning and teach the vep of the thon. There is such a house every six miles along the canal. This one is only half a mile from here, across the bridge. This is the Elder Dlan, head of the House. He will arrange—"

"I got the message," I said. "O.K., tell the Headmaster I'd like to see his school."

As soon as we went outside, the tomb-like chill of the mayoralty gave place to pleasant warmth. It was high morning, with the little yellow sun blazing out of that deep blue cloudless sky, and I guessed the temperature was about 20 Celsius, and rising. This was the beginning of autumn, but thon 2-3-0 lay only about 15° south, so the sun would pass quite close to the zenith at noon, and in fact it would soon be damned hot. I stripped off my padded robe, re-buckled my laser on my uniform, and left my former overcoat with one of Tlavei's children.

As people milled around, and the elders summoned a thapal-carriage, I asked Saimo about dates within the year. She told me today was Day 4 of First Month—for the Xuman calendar year began with the northern spring or southern autumn equinox. The system seemed geared to the northern hemisphere because Xuman civilization had originally centered in the north—now it was more equatorial. There were six days in a *heran* ("handful" or "week"), and the weekdays were named after *fingers*—every sixth day (*pedan*: "thumb") was a half-holiday, and every twelfth (*pedandav,* "second thumb") a full holiday. But today we were only on the fourth finger, so it was a full working day.

It certainly looked like it. From the mayoralty entrance we had a good view of the main road, which was now fairly crowded with traffic—mostly thapal-carriages. These came in many sizes, designs, and colors, but all looked neat and beautiful—even the four-thapal carts laden with bales or barrels, the heavy cargo-trucks of Xuma.

Saimo pointed to a red-painted cart. "That is from Nakaan, a subject-city of Xarth," she said. "The Xarthians are our enemies, they are always raiding us, but this is the Road of Peace, on it there is perpetual truce for the sake of trade. In fact, all this west side of the canal should be free of raids, it is the Death Side, and the hudaan are specially sacred. Yesterday for the first time the Xarthians broke this custom. But it is like their ruler to do so, I think—that emperor Retumon is a vile beast . . ."

I mentally filed that one: a point to us. If the Xarthians had violated the local war code, then we had a good case for some unorthodox reprisals . . .

Now our carriage came alongside. It was painted white and yellow, the colors of the Elders, and the driver too was grey-skinned, white-robed, and yellow-haired. He/she jerked the reins, and we were quickly away, trotting along the Road of Peace towards the bridge.

Zai, Saimo's mother, was sharing the front seat with

the elder Dlan, while I shared the back seat with Saimo. I could see that Saimo was a little upset at the coolness of the welcome she had got from her mother, but she was bravely mastering her feelings, for this kind of detachment from former ties was normal among Xuman elders, and young people knew they had to put up with it when the time came. I pressed Saimo's slim fingers, and looked over the stone balustrade of the bridge.

The waters of that canal were a misty blue. On it for a long way northwards—in fact, for as far as the eye could reach—there was a traffic of small boats, only a little sparser than the wheeled traffic of the Road of Peace. Most were quite small, and propelled by paddlers, men or children; but one craft that shot out from under the bridge had a black-and-red long slim hull and a lateen sail—it made me think of a cross between a Venetian gondola and a Greek galley. It was loaded with bales along its centerline; Saimo said it was a trader heading for Lylaxa in the far north.

Gazing at the misty blue waters, I suddenly noticed, almost simultaneously, that one small boat had lines lowered over the side, and below the surface there were streaks of what looked like red fire.

"Water-movers," said Saimo. "They are not bright now—you should see them in the spring. Then they have real light of their own, when they are mating."

I soon worked out that the "water-movers" were *fish*. They were about the size of large goldfish.

"There are bigger kinds, too, but not so pretty," explained Saimo. "Those are the ones we catch and eat. Not these little fire-fish. They are for beauty only."

"Where did they come from in the first place—before you had any canals?" I asked.

Saimo was silent, but the elder Dlan turned to me.

"In the time before the Order, there were flowing waters and standing waters upon Xuma—sweet waters as well as salt. When those waters died away, we Elders saved what we could of the water life, and established it in the canals."

"Don't they foul up the system?" I said. "Your pumps, your dams . . .?"

"We have devices to protect them," said Dlan ambiguously—I think he meant "protect the fish" as much as "protect the machinery."

"One other point," I said. "We used to have stories, many years ago, about a planet like yours, very dry, with canals. Most of us were quite sure the canals would have to be covered up completely, like tubes, to prevent loss of water into the air. How comes it that your canals are open ones?"

Dlan smiled. "In the beginning, we tried the system you mention. We used the dried trunks of *tula*-plants, which held the water—but they held it too well. The tubes would not maintain fish, and the air over the canal areas became too dry for comfort of animal life. So we gave up the tubes. The open canals are better in every way. Especially, they are more beautiful."

I had to grant him that. With its blue waters, its firefish, its shipping, and its stone banks and pagoda-like houses on either side, beautiful that canal certainly was.

Then we were past the canal, and speeding eastwards into the countryside, along a road shaded by those fan-like *kaal* trees. Our thapal stepped very high with his absurd spindly legs on the stone-paved road, and yet the ride was quite comfortable. Saimo told me this carriage was a superior model, with flexible metal springs and tires of some rubbery substance.

"There is air inside," she said.

Pneumatic tires! The Xumans' technology was not all that primitive, then. Well, over 2 million years there had to be *some* progress, after all. They were still in the horse-and-buggy stage; but their buggies were advanced types.

The scenery on either side of the avenue was much like what I had seen the previous day on the west side of the canal—fields of bluish reeds or grass or various crops, interspersed with tufts of trees and isolated farmers' houses. There were a lot of red-skinned workers in the fields or filing along the road, most of them naked children or kilted men. Certainly the Xumans had not mechanized their agriculture. As we passed them, the peasants on the road bowed low to the elders in the front seats.

I now felt confident of the general setup of Xuman civilization: it had to be something like ancient China, with a dash of old Egypt or medieval Europe thrown in. As we rode along, I kept questioning Saimo and Dlan, and their answers confirmed this picture. Respect for age, for elders, for old customs—yes, they had all that. The four age/sex groups were a hierarchy: sexless Elders were the most respected, then women, then men, then children. But the Elders were not exactly part of the body politic—they belonged to the Order, a great planet-wide church which stood apart from all national states, with lesser and greater schools and monasteries strung out along the canals, planted in every city, and established strongly in the sub-Arctic and sub-Antarctic wastes where huge dams gathered the life-giving waters for the whole world every spring. The entire canal system was in their charge, and about half the whole population of Elders were basically tenders of canals. Others acted as schoolmasters to the thons and counsellors to the governments of cities; the greatest minds among them mostly went to "the cold places," the polar monasteries. Dlan himself was a more important person than I had thought: he was not merely a schoolmaster, but rather more like a medieval abbot, since he was the chief of all the elders in 2-3-0 and the two neighboring thons.

Both Elders and canals were sacrosanct: neither were ever injured in war, not even by such reckless tyrants as the Emperor of Xarth. For it was on the skills and wisdom of the Elders that the life of the planet depended.

"But power in the cities?" I said. "Do you Elders hold that?"

Dlan smiled. "No. We leave such amusements to younger souls. In Yelsai and in most of Middle and West Sectors, it is women who hold the power, because they are older and fewer than men. In some cities of the East, also in Xarth, it is *kurar* who are the rulers."

"*Kurar?*"

"Pervert men," said Dlan grimly. "You know, a few of our people go through the sex stages the wrong way round. They begin as *kynthi*, and then they turn into *kurar*—old men! The Emperor of Xarth was once the dancing-girl Retumon, a concubine of the previous Emperor. That sort are the most vicious. They lust for power, they love to dominate both women and *kynthi*, and they avenge their earlier condition by acts of insane violence. I hold that men should never be rulers—it is their nature to be fighting animals. I am glad it is long, long since I was a man."

Saimo and I looked at each other guiltily. Each of us was an offense to the ideals of this old neuter.

Dlan seemed to guess at least part of my thought. He added:

"Of course, with gods it is no doubt different. You, god Tomass, must combine the force of a man with infinite wisdom and infinite benevolence—as our ancient stories would lead us to expect. But ordinary, mortal men—they make things so much worse for themselves! In rivalry—especially rivalry for women—they kill each other; and the more they kill each other, the fewer there are left to become women at the end of their twenty-four years. The common soldiers of all armies on Xuma are men, though most generals are women since one needs experience and caution to be a general. In some countries—Xarth, for instance—there are more than twice as many males as females. The disproportion is not so bad in Yelsai, because here the law allows women of all ranks to take two husbands."

"Because?" I said. "I don't follow."

"In Xarth, since the perverts seized power, ordinary women are allowed only one husband. This makes for a lot of unsatisfied males, which makes for more rivalry and more killing among males, and so finally a still worse disproportion. To straighten out the mess in Xarth, they would have to allow women three husbands for several generations. But the Emperor of Xarth likes things the way they are, because of course *he* can have as many females as he wants, and he is able to lead his frustrated soldiers into wars of aggression. That raid yesterday, god Tomass—if you had not been there, they would have slaughtered all the males on the west side of the thon, and raped all the females before carrying them off as slaves. That is how they behave all the time . . ."

"Nasty guys," I said. "It would be a good idea to conquer them once and for all, wouldn't it?"

Dlan looked at me narrowly. "That is a political question—not one for a humble village Elder like me to answer. You will talk to the Queen about that, no? But you surprise me, my lord god. You are doubtless very wise; but how can 'once' be 'for all'? All things come round."

We got into a tangle on this one, and it took a couple of minutes before we were straightened out. I was amazed to find that the Xumans believed time was *circular*.

"I am sure you understand this perfectly already," said Dlan blandly, "for it was the gods who taught us this wisdom in the first place. But since you playfully pretend ignorance, I will expound the doctrine as we have received it. As every *xir* (linc; canal) is really part of a great *xirux* (circle), so with time. The circumference is doubtless very great—millions of millions of years—but in the end the future returns as the past, What will be, was; what was, will be."

"So everything is fixed already," I said.

"No, everything is forever free," said Dlan. "That is why we are eternally responsible."

I gave up. This sort of philosophy was not in my line. I guessed they debated this sort of thing in their monasteries from the north pole to the south pole—it sounded as if it could have kept them happy for a couple of million years, during which time we low-browed Earthmen had gone from chipped flints to starships.

"We are there," said Dlan. "The Gold-and-Silver House."

I saw ahead of us a large building of white stone with a yellow tiled roof. It had a small forecourt, and behind that on either side of the building there went out a long low bank covered with strange vegetation. The blue-green plant—possibly a single continuous plant—was all tubes with runners half a meter thick creeping over that bank and diving into it; equally thick rising stems soared to enormous circular leaves some five meters above ground. Here and there slimmer risers terminated not in leaves but in orange conical meter-wide flowers at about the height of a man's head. The array of these leaves and flowers, like a strip of giant nasturtiums, carried along that bank on both sides of the Gold-and-Silver House northwards and southwards as far as the eye could see.

"That is the *tula*," said Dlan; "the name is from *tul*, to communicate. Its dried leaves give us paper for writing; and its stems hold water, as I said; also other useful things. Come now, let us get down."

We did so; and then Saimo and her mother said goodbye to each other. Zai had to go back to her own thon's monastery six miles away.

"My former child," she said, "I think you will be going a longer journey. May your voyagings be for the good of Xuma!"

Chapter Four

I guess the first thing which really jolted my complacency about the relative levels of human and Xuman civilization was—what I learned about their linguistics. I suppose this is how things usually happen: the expert is only impressed by expertise in his own field.

They showed me all over that monastery-school. It was much as I had expected, at first glance, very tasteful, very bare. There were no children around, because the classes for them were given only in the early mornings, and by now they were all out working in the fields; but quite a few grey-skinned neuters were in evidence, for instance in the library and scriptorium.

The Xumans, I found, wrote only by hand, forming letter after letter by a technique akin to drawing—an art we Euram Earthmen lost about in the middle of the 21st Century. I believe my grandparents could still *write*, in that sense; and some of the Chinks on the lunar Far Side still can, I'm told; but all other civilized men long ago came to rely on machines, either dictos or (for special purposes) the more laborious typers. I already knew that Saimo could "write": even in *Riverhorse* the kid had amazed us with mysterious squiggles

when we had lent him/her a drawing machine; and
now I saw the art being practiced in all its archaic
glory. I watched, fascinated, as the Xuman scribes
dipped their reed pens in the blue and orange inks, and
rapidly, gracefully, traced lines of curving script on the
cream-colored *tula* paper.

"Have you ever thought of, ah, *printing?*" I said,
using the English word.

Saimo explained to the Abbot.

"Oh, that," said Dlan carelessly. "Yes, it is noted in
our annals that we used that method widely up to about
the year *kolaz* [about 20,000]. After that we discarded
it except for special purposes—it led to preservation of
too much trivia. Now we cultivate penmanship as a fine
art, and use *exact reproduction* only for the official
chronicle and for approved masterpieces. The only
reproducing press in the world is kept at Khadan."

"Khadan?" I said feebly.

"The Place-of-Dams at the south end of the canal
system. That is where the official chronicler and the Supreme Court of Poetry reside."

I inquired about the writing system, and about
Xuman languages—and was utterly amazed.

There was now only one Xuman language currently
spoken by all nations, and it was written in a perfectly
beautiful and perfectly phonetic script, which however
came in two varieties—monumental and cursive; the
first looked vaguely like Greek, the second like Arabic
or vintage shorthand. As Dlan demonstrated the letters,
I saw that their forms implied a perfect phonetic analysis of speech sounds—but that was not all. For the Abbot proceeded to show me written specimens of 673
known dead Xuman languages, 27 of them world-lan-
guages directly ancestral to the present-day Xuman.
The present Xuman had been current, with almost no
variation of time or national dialect, for some half-mil-
lion years.

"How do you manage that?" I gasped. "I can't read
anything easily in my own language that's older than
about 500 years. Language naturally changes—"

"Language naturally corrupts," said Dlan severely.
"There is no *need* for change unless new objects are in-

troduced into the system of life, and even then the need
is only for new vocabulary. We stabilized our language
half a million years ago in its most perfect form by
means of linguistic analysis and certain teaching
methods. The theory is as follows . . ."

Our conversation went on for about an hour: poor
Saimo was hard put to it to help me out with my grop-
ing questions. By the time I half understood Dlan, I
was sweating, partly because the day was warming up,
but mainly because I was embarrassed and ashamed.
These hidebound conservatives, these medieval mystics,
had passed the stage of Bloomfield two million years
ago, Chomsky not long after, and Wedeker, Mboto,
Rao et al—all our 21st and 22nd Century performation-
ists—dead at the starting-gate at least a million years
back. Especially on semantics, Dlan had me grov-
elling. I certainly did not understand fully, partly because my grasp of the language was inadequate, but
largely because my grasp of *language*, the philosophy of
communication itself, was rudimentary compared with
that of this Xuman village abbot.

I made a mental resolution. *Afterwards*, when we
had established our power over Xuma, and things were
settled and peaceful, I would make a study trip to
Khadan, to meet the "real linguists," as Dlan called
them. And then I would publish—via interstellar radio—a monograph that would revolutionize human
linguistics. That is, if there was still any human linguistics left on Luna to revolutionize.

Dlan, all the while, regarded me mildly but inscruta-
bly. From time to time he asked polite questions about
"divine" linguistics.

"So," he said, intrigued at one of my remarks, "you
still have *three* current languages among the gods! Is
that for religious-mystical reasons, my lord? The Triune
symbol?"

"Well," I said weakly, "no, not quite. I guess it's to
make communication more difficult."

"Ah," said Dlan, nodding sagely, "I see: you have
too much goodness among you, no? Evil too has its
rights, yes; how marvellous, that you are so good you

68

have to work at being evil in order to maintain manifestation!"

"Er—look," I said, "I think it's time I was on my way to see the Queen."

"Certainly," said the Abbot. "We have made some preliminary arrangements already. Actually, you have a choice of several means of transport, depending on how fast you feel you must travel. The slowest but most comfortable would be by sailboat along the canal; the quickest we can offer you would be on thapal-back. Between those extremes there is wheeled carriage or towed *gola*. But—"

At this point my attention was distracted. The scriptorium was on an upper floor and had wide windows facing east. While Dlan was still speaking, I happened to glance out of a window. Beyond the monastery area lay a wood of palm-like trees, and beyond that again some high posts rising well above the green fronds— posts that were joined to each other by a wide-meshed net. The posts and the netting extended indefinitely north and south. I had noticed them before and assumed that they had some agricultural purpose—it was not they which now caught my eye.

Just above the net and the wood there was now rising into the air a large round balloon. It was much like the contraptions pictured in the history books of Earth's Nineteenth Century, except that below the huge globe was slung not a simple square basket, but a car shaped like a little ship, with a pointed prow and stern. There were lateral sail-like projections joining the car and the globe, and obviously stabilizing the craft so that the prow of the "ship" pointed in the direction of movement.

As there seemed to be a steady east wind, the whole contraption was coming towards us. While I watched, the balloon-ship floated majestically up and over the monastery. I saw little red figures leaning over the side of the car.

"That is a *gola*," said Dlan. "They are the flying ships of Xuma, and they are mostly used for east-west trade. That one, by its colors, is from Peral Ao (East Sector). It will float with the trade wind to Peral Xúl

(West Sector), and so on home, round the world, since the wind always blows from the east in this middle belt of Xuma. I was saying that if you wish to, you could ride to Yelsai in the car of a *gola*—but the *gola* would have to be towed low over the ground by thapals, for the wind will not serve north to south. There is a regular tow-path beyond that net, and the net and the path run all along the east side of the canal, because, you realize, golas cannot navigate very accurately—they usually hit a canal-net and are then towed to the city of their destination. But, my lord, if you are in something of a hurry—"

"I am, rather," I said.

"Then surely your quickest method would be to get back into your own divine flier, and take it to Yelsai, according to directions which we or the military can supply to you."

At that moment another elder came up, bowed to Dlan, and spoke a few rapid sentences. Dlan turned to me.

"The military are here now. Would you like to see them?"

"Sure," I said.

In the yard before the building we found the troops of Yelsai, some two dozen infantry and a dozen cavalry. They were basically similar in appearance to the Xarthian raiders, but less terrifying, since their helmets covered only the tops and backs of their heads, and they had no skull-masks; all were armed with swords, and the foot soldiers also carried spears. A mounted standard-bearer displayed the pennon of Yelsai—a golden fire-fish on a blue background.

Next to him, the leader of the troops now dismounted from his thapal. He was distinguished by a gilded helmet with a blue plume; yet he was a man. After less than 24 hours on Xuma, this already struck me as unusual—so far, every person of high status had been either a woman or a neuter elder.

The man-leader raised both his palms to the sides of his helmet in what I took to be a salute; for good measure, he also bowed to Dlan and myself. Then he addressed me. His voice was deeper than any I had yet heard on this planet: a good musical bass.

"Great high god," he said, "we wretched killer-folk have taken the liberty of placing a guard upon your excellent bird-machine, lest the killer-folk of Xarth should ride again that way and attempt to do it harm. I hope we have acted rightly."

"Your men have not touched it, I hope?" I said. "There are dangerous magics built into it. Anyone who tries to enter it may be struck dead."

"We guessed that. I gave strict orders that no warrior should approach the metal bird within ten fathoms. Most of the guard will be much farther off than that, riding patrols through the Desert of Death to watch for Xarthians. The godly bird is safe, O descender from Vepan."

I felt abashed. This officer had shown a certain cool sense, whereas I should have thought of my booby-trapped lander before. We were close to the Xarthian frontier in this district, and I could not safely leave the machine where it was. I made my decision.

"I will fly to Yelsai with my interpreter," I said, "that is, if you can show me where to land."

"Gladly," said the officer. "The best place is the city field on the east side of Yelsai, where the trading golas come down or are towed to their sheds. There are many facilities there for the reception of air travellers."

"The *airport*," I said in English. "Of course! Why didn't I think of that before?"

We went back into the building and Dlan and his elders brought me maps. They were beautifully drawn in inks of many colors; they corresponded pretty exactly to the photo maps in my lander, but were much more detailed and written up with local information.

"I can't read the words on them," I said.

"But I can, master," said Saimo. "I will guide you, my lord."

Before we left for the desert, Saimo and I lunched at the monastery; and just after the meal I radioed my news to *Riverhorse*. Dlan eyed me with interest as I spoke into the metal and plastic of my collar. At one point I had to bring him into the conversation.

"The gods on high wish to know," I said, "whether anyone will be ready to receive me in Yelsai. By your methods, the news of my arrival couldn't have got there yet."

"I beg to correct you, my lord god," said the Abbot. "The news has already reached Yelsai, and the Queen awaits you."

"But it's 300 miles," I exclaimed. "What do you use? Drums? Smoke signals?"

Dlan smiled. "There are several methods. The younger folk—the females and males—they use such things as flashing mirrors—we have nearly always good strong sunshine. At night, one can make lights to wink. For written messages, the soldiers maintain relays of thapals. I will not go into all the details, my lord, but I can assure you that when you reach Yelsai flying field you will receive a *royal* welcome."

I translated this information for Mannheim. He seemed alarmed.

"Carson, keep your eyes open," he ordered. "I was going to propose that we land many more personnel, now that it's clear humans can survive on the surface, eat the food, and so on—"

"Thank you," I said.

"—but now I'd rather wait another day or two. Keep your eyes open, and report regularly! Those redskins are more advanced than we realized. What are those balloons filled with, for chrissake?"

"Helium. They get it from natural gas, I'm told."

"*Helium.* There you are. Carson, if you were more of a chemist, you'd realize how much technology it takes to extract *helium* from natural gas. We could only do it ourselves about two-and-a-half centuries ago. How long have these redskins been doing it?"

"About a million years."

"Yet they're still fighting wars with bows and arrows. Carson, I don't like the smell of this. Hell, it stinks! Stinks of helium, or something. O.K., you go to Yelsai and see this Queen. Find out more about their technology, and about their power structure. At that, we might send down a couple more guys to reinforce you soon—say, a chemist and a sociologist."

"If you send anyone, how about Sally Freeston and Dave Weiser? Sally's got a degree in chemy, org and inorg, and Dave has the socio. Also, Sally speaks some Xuman."

"We'll consider that," said Mannheim unenthusiastically. "Meanwhile, will you please use your eyes, Carson—and your head?"

After I had turned down the volume I realized that Mannheim was asking me to play the part of a spy. Well, why not? Wasn't I already doing so? I hadn't avoided the spooks' brigade after all—I had merely joined the interstellar section.

Saimo touched my hand. "If you are ready, master, shall we go?"

It was the hottest part of the afternoon when we returned to the western desert. It would have been murder to walk, but luckily the military had arranged for me to ride on a thapal. I couldn't have stayed on the brute's back by myself, since I had never ridden any animal in my whole life—the only horses on the Moon are in Lunaris zoo—but the warrior captain Zav placed me in front of him on his own mount, and I hung onto the beast's long neck while Zav held onto me. Saimo rode another thapal all by herself, with an ease and grace which impressed me—apparently she had learned to ride when still a little kid.

As we passed the line of hudaan, I had to hang on grimly to the thapal's neck, for the beast was jogging up and down a lot over the uneven ground. I suddenly realized that Zav, from behind me, could easily draw my laser from its holster, and in spite of the heat I felt a sudden chill. Hanging on with my left hand, I clapped my right to my hip.

Zav seemed to guess my thoughts. "Have no fear, great god," he said, "your magic weapon will not fall out of its sheath from that position: I checked that as soon as we began riding."

I felt sheepish. Obviously, Zav had no intention of beating me to the draw. I began to like him.

"Zav," I said, "so far, of all the Xuman folk I have seen, you are the most like a male god—the most like me. The other Xuman men are more like boys."

Zav said gruffly, "I am not a man."

"What?"

"Not a *kunir*—I am a *kurar*, a pervert male. When I was younger I was a plaything of the soldiers on the frontier. Now I command a few of them. This is the normal career of such as I in Yelsai—if one can use the word 'normal' about us at all. We commonly rise to captain's rank (*kavyo*), sometimes even to colonel (*hazyo*). But the higher officers are all women." He laughed. "If male gods are like *kurar*, then perhaps you will do well in Yelsai, my lord Tomass."

"Why?"

"Queen Telesin is somewhat partial to *kurar*. According to rumor, young normal boys do not satisfy her. She is a great lady, our Queen, and always on the look-out for new and vigorous lovers. She has no objection at all to foreigners. For instance, the last ambassador from Xiriko . . ."

"What happened to him?"

"He left last month. Exhausted, they say, even though he was a tough, healthy *kurar*. At present Her Majesty has no established favorite . . ."

I felt hot once again.

PART TWO

God and Queen

Chapter Five

When we emerged from the lander on the airfield of Yelsai, the whole situation seemed oddly familiar.

By now I was used to Xuman gravity, and I came quickly down the steps after Saimo, facing forwards. I had put the astroplane down on a field of short grass-weed, just before a stone-paved area with a line of two-storyed buildings beyond. Around and behind us there were balloon-ships moored or being maneuvered near masts, nets and sheds by a lot of red-skinned Xumans. And just before the main entrance of the central building ahead, I saw a group of people who radiated expectation.

Then I realized—it was all rather like arriving at one of our home space-ports—well, in essence, and barring the fact that the sky here was blue, not black, and so on. I looked at Saimo, and smiled.

"We'd better go meet the reception committee," I said in English.

Saimo looked a bit nervous. "I—I think the Queen herself is here," she said.

The afternoon was still warm as we strode forward, but there was a softer feeling to the air of Yelsai, as though there was more moisture in it, and life might be less of a struggle here against death and deserts. We had not far to walk, and now the Xuman party was coming to meet us.

At once I knew which was Queen Telesin. She was tall (for a Xuman) and very handsome. No, I'd better be honest—I thought her beautiful. You know how it is with strange races—the Chinks, for example—it takes your eyes a bit of time to get adjusted. For a while they all look alike; and then they *don't.*

Telesin's eyes were the first thing that struck me about her—they were not yellowish, but pure bright green. (I learned later that green eyes were rare on the West Canal, but not so uncommon in Telesin's native district, which bordered on the territory of the next city to the southeast, namely Tlanash.) The green eyes made her look slightly more human—she almost reminded me of Sally—but no human eyes were quite so vivid: against her smooth red skin they sparkled like emeralds. She wore her black hair over her ears, and that hid the unhumanness of them, so that really at first glance she might have passed for a very striking human girl, if you didn't count her fingers.

In that first glance, I wasn't counting her fingers.

She was dressed basically like mayoress Tlavei had been, in a high-collared green gown which left her conical breasts exposed. But her gown was of a finer linen than Tlavei's, so that you could see the lines of her body through it. She wore golden sandals and gold bracelets, and on her glossy black hair a gold circlet from which hung a row of flashing jewels—emeralds, rubies, sapphires. The jewels on her forehead were emeralds, which perfectly matched her eyes.

It was only afterwards that I learnt that the crown of Yelsai was not hereditary, and queens were chosen largely for their *beauty.*

"*Kelnei xipui Yelsai, aanir tlavol,*" said Telesin in a clear warm soprano—a voice like honey and fire and flutes. I knew all those words, in theory; but it took me a second or two to gather my wits. The Queen had said "Welcome to Yelsai, good god"; and all I could think was, good god!

Finally I stammered, "I did not know Xuman queens could be so beautiful."

This speech apparently went down extremely well. Telesin smiled.

"I see even gods can be diplomats. I am used to flattery, but you do it very well. Now let me introduce the others. This is my child Varan—you see he wears a kilt, for he changed two months ago, and that will tell you what an old woman I am."

I thought Varan was a strong handsome boy, if a bit serious-looking: he was about Saimo's height, but broader in the shoulders. Poor Saimo! She too would have become a fine young man but for me ... and now she was looking sad and lost.

The Queen went on. "And now let me introduce two of my counsellors—the elders Kanyo and Psyl. They have one claim to fame in the world of Xuma since the ninth month of last year—it was they who first saw your star Vepan enter our skies, for one of their scholarly interests is astronomy. I suppose Psyl was the very first person in our world to notice you ..."

I looked at the two white-robed elders. There was something different about their eyes, too, that greyskinned couple: yes, they both had dark brown irises.

"Where are you from?" I asked.

"We should rather ask that of you," said Psyl, with a quick smile. "As it happens, sir god, we are not natives of Yelsai—when we were male and female we were of Xulpona, in the West Sector. But elders wander to many places, and mostly shed old loyalties ..."

"May we ask," said Kanyo earnestly, "from what world do you come, sir? We are sure that Vepan is too small to be a world in itself, too small, for one thing, to hold onto its air—"

"You'd be surprised," I said, "it *is* pretty much of a world."

"Perhaps the air is *inside*," said Psyl.

I did not quite know what to say. Oddly enough, the Xumans up the canal had asked very few questions about us Earth folk; and now that fact came home to me forcibly at the quizzing of these two old astronomers. Of course, I wasn't going to hide the basic facts;

in any case, Saimo knew them. But I thought these were matters we had better discuss in conditions of greater secrecy. My experiences back home on Luna made me wonder if the Xarthians or other foreign powers might not have their spooks at this airport . . .

"And who is this—this—" began the Queen, looking at Saimo.

"—boy?" I added hastily. "He is my interpreter."

"You hardly need that," said Telesin, smiling graciously at me. "But I remember now—this is the kid you napped, and then brought back, and then overnight the shock made the little one change. Very well, Saimo—you are welcome, along with your master. And now, let us go to the Palace."

I noticed that the Queen had not referred to Saimo as "boy" (*kunir*) or "he" (*luir*).

Yelsai is a city of hardly more than 100,000 people, but it covers a fairly large area, since it is full of gardens, parks, plazas, minor canals and artificial lakes, and few buildings are more than three stories high. Its plan is a bellied-out triangle, for it stands at the junction of three great canals, and branches of those canals form a moat all round the yellow stone city wall. The city's name means "Six Gates": at each gate there is a wide bridge over the moat. The balloon-port lies outside the wall and moat near the northeast gate, the Gate of Dragons: here there is a small suburb, populated largely by travellers and balloon crews. But the royal palace stands in the heart of Yelsai itself, so we now had a fairly lengthy journey to make through the city streets.

We travelled in a procession of magnificent open thapal-coaches, and I got a vivid tourist's impression of the city. It was a cheerful, colorful place, and its ambience was different from that of thon 2-3-0 because there was more commercial bustle. In general you could say that the state of Yelsai ran a system which mixed commune socialism and private enterprise: in the country the socialism predominated, but in the city it was the other way round. There were a lot of people selling food and charcoal and trinkets, some from boats on the canals, some on the streets—the street vendors were mostly naked children who roamed the avenues or the sides of the canals crying their wares in musical voices—when two or three of them were peddling in the same street the effect was like a madrigal.

But the serious shopping centered in the market squares; there are three of these, and we passed one, the Market of Whirling Stars, which is famous for jewelry and pretty girls. Under the shady *kaal* trees, the orderly stalls made a brilliant display of color—especially the fruit and cloth stalls. I suddenly remembered a piece of history I had once read—an old conquistador's description of the market square of Tenochtitlan, which he first entered like me as an honored guest. In that market of Old Mexico, too, there had been "dealers in gold, silver, and precious stones, feathers, cloaks, and embroidered goods . . ." But one thing was very different: no stalls for "male and female slaves." Private slavery did not exist in Yelsai: though "perverts" were in bondage to the state, no one was ever bought or sold.

I learned some of these points during our drive to the palace; but it was not easy to be a tourist: there were—distractions. Saimo and I had been placed in the Queen's coach along with a couple of young male warriors who, I learned, were *dan kunaya,* royal guardsmen. When we got in Telesin made the guards sit beside Saimo, and patted the vacant place right beside herself.

"For you, my lord god," she smiled.

One of the young guardsmen tried to protest. "My Queen, he has a magic weapon—"

"I know," said Telesin coolly. "That is why he is here, boy! His weapon is much stronger than yours, and I will have him show it to me later. He has brought it to Yelsai to serve me with it—what else? Haven't you?" she said, turning to me.

"Well—" I stammered. "Your majesty, don't you think we ought to discuss these matters in private?"

"Oh, the whole city knows what I do even before I do it," she said; "that is what Queens are for, anyway—to cause agreeable scandal. So what is the use of being coy?"

I began to be bewildered. I wasn't sure what the conversation was supposed to be about. After a minute or so, Telesin leaned forward and said something rapidly to Saimo. "Interpret," she added.

"Our lady Queen," said Saimo, blushing, "she says you are more handsome even than her last favorite, and she says if you are a man or a *kurar*."

"Well, can't you explain, Saimo?"

Saimo looked at me pitifully. "My lord, I never did know. The lady Sally once told me that you and she were about the same age, but which was *kurar* or *kynthi* I never found out."

Of course; I should have realized. There were no children aboard *Riverhorse*, and Xuman men and women look much the same age even though they are not. How could poor Saimo guess at our biology? Every being thinks his own race is normal; and all Xuman vertebrates go through the four-stage sex cycle—separate sexes on Xuma occur only in fire-fish (which are invertebrate chordates) and lower organisms. For all that Saimo could tell the authorities of Yelsai, we humans still had one enormous secret—that we were sexed like worms or fire-fish. And I did not know what the Xumans' reaction would be when they learned the truth.

I decided to stall. "Saimo," I said, "Sally is a normal woman of our people."

Saimo looked as though she wanted to kiss me, but of course dared not. In English she said: "Dear Tomass, if it does not grieve you, then I am glad. So you will not despise me!" Then she turned to the Queen, and blurted out what she thought was my secret.

The Queen beamed. "I thought as much. *Kurar* are so much more experienced—more truly *male*! My dear god, I am sure we are going to be great friends . . ."

It was then that we reached the Market of Whirling Stars, and I hurriedly began asking the Queen a tourist's questions. Unfortunately, my questions seemed to bring the conversation back onto the same subject.

"It is named for the Whirling Stars," said Telesin, "because *Whirling Stars* has the by-meaning of *dancers*. Those girls who sell the jewels are mostly kynthi, with some normal women who are dancers at the pleasure houses. The jewel merchants are happy to employ them as sellers by day, and the girls are happy too because the work is light and pleasant; they can meet all their friends there, and the customers who buy the jewels often turn up at night at the pleasure houses to buy something else. I should know," she added, with a little laugh.

"Why?" I said, astonished.

"Because I was one of them, once. Ah, Tomass, how many years ago! When I turned woman, my husband—he was a *kurar* captain, bless him—my husband brought me from my thon to the big city, and trained me as a dancer. *He* had had experience of that when he was with the army, so his training was excellent . . . I was very popular, Tomass, let me tell you, in those days, and that is how I was elected Queen—so many of the young men knew me and liked me. I used to sell jewels by day, and by night I danced at the House of the Spring Fire-Fish—ah, here it is, the dear old place . . ."

We had come to a square which was mostly filled with a garden and an ornamental lake; on the other side of the lake stood a long low building with a flared red roof. The general effect was rather like pictures I had seen of Japanese temples. Around the House of the Fire-Fish I saw couples or groups of people sitting on the grass under the spreading kaal trees—kilted men and bejewelled, bare-breasted girls in half-length skirts.

"This is merely the hour to drink *tlaok*," smiled Telesin; "the serious business will begin later. As it will for us, my lord god . . ."

The Palace lay on the south side of the great main city square. It was a complex of platforms, towers, and above all gardens—sunken gardens, raised gardens, even roof gardens. Some of the tower-like blocks had pagoda-type flared roofs of blue tiles, others had flat roofs surrounded by balustrades; and there seemed to be vegetation everywhere. Flowering creepers swarmed up the yellow stone walls, little jungles of tula spilled over the parapets. The Queen's apartments, in which

Saimo and I were given a room, formed an ample penthouse block on the main flat roof of the central tower. Outside our windows lay a magnificent roof garden.

"How do they keep all these plants irrigated up here?" I asked Saimo as we settled in.

"The elders arrange that," she said. "The royal gardeners are all *uxan,* and they have machines to raise water from the lakes and canals. The elders arrange many things in Yelsai."

"Do they arrange what the Queen will do about peace or war?"

"Not 'arrange'—they only advise. The acts of the state are decided by the Queen and her Twelve Ladies . . ."

I went on quizzing Saimo, and at last got a fairly clear idea of the setup. The Twelve Ladies were at once a Cabinet and a Parliament—they were representatives of the people, or rather of the women, for only normal women, *kun,* had votes. Each Lady represented a sector of the city or the surrounding canals, and she held her position as long as she remained a woman. As "Ladies" were usually fairly mature when elected—they were normally ex-mayoresses—their terms of office were not often more than a half-dozen years. Queens lasted longer, because they were chosen from *young* normal women—and chosen in a sort of beauty contest by a panel of young *men* (the only occasion on which men exercised any political power). Both Ladies and Queens of course retired when they turned Elder, because throughout Xuma this third Change was legally a death ("the First Death"). So, for instance, Queen Telesin's husband had "died" a dozen years ago and was now an elder in Khadan. Telesin herself had already reigned 18 years.

Political power was shared between the Queen and her body of Ladies; on all important matters the Queen and the Ladies had to agree or no action would be taken. Among themselves, the Ladies could decide by a majority vote, but usually they preferred to be unanimous.

"A good system for stopping anything being done," I said. "Are all the states of Xuma governed this way?"

"No, master," said Saimo, "there are many different

systems. Tlanash has no Queen, but only nine Ladies. In the eastern cities there are hereditary monarchs and the ruler can inherit while still a child and keep the throne when becoming first a man and then a woman. In Xarth, for many years now only *kurar* rule, and the power of the *Alkayo,* the Emperor, is absolute for life or death, for peace or war. In the West—"

"O.K., spare me the details," I said. "I get the picture. Tell me, Saimo, how strong is that place Xarth?"

"Too strong," she said, with a shudder. "All my life, we of the West Canal thons have feared the Xarthians. The North Wall lies at thon 2-5-0. Beyond that formerly the canal belonged to Nakaan, a peaceful city, but now all Nakaan has been swallowed by Xarth. First the Emperor had only the one city of Xarth, now he holds three, and he still wants more. He would like to rule all this Middle Sector, I think—that is why our Queen has made alliance with Tlanash against him."

"Are there bigger empires—say, in the East?"

"There are richer ones," said Saimo. "For instance, Kvaryla, Aosai, and Idaxir—but I think none controls more than two main cities, and they are all jealous of each other and not dangerous to the rest of the world. They like more to amass wealth by their trading *golas* than to send forth armies. And the West Sector is peaceful. No, there is nothing very like Xarth elsewhere on the face of Xuma—and in my thon school I remember our elder taught us that there has been none such for the past 20,000 years."

I put my hands on Saimo's shoulders, and kissed her on the forehead. "Well, my dear, if your Queen and Ladies are sensible, we can put an end to the Xarthian menace. With the power of us sky 'gods,' we could wipe out their whole Empire in minutes, just as I wiped out those raiders. If the Queen asks you, will you tell her that, eh?"

Saimo's lips trembled. "I do not think the Queen will ask *me* about *you,* Tomass. At the great feast tonight I am sure she will do business with you directly. Tomass, I have been thinking—"

"About what? Go on, my dear."

"About love," she said, blushing slightly. "Tomass, I

85

have already told you that I love you. If you wish me, I
am your slave-girl forever. I do not ask more than that
you be kind to me, as you have always been. I know
you gods come from a far and glorious world where
you have enormous powers—in the circle of life you
are closer to the center of things, to us Xumans you are
like Elders and to you we are all like *vep*. For you to
feel ordinary love for a Xuman—that is not to be expected, and I do not expect it—"

"Oh, come on, Saimo," I protested, "that's nonsense!"

"No, it is not nonsense, my dear master: it is truth. I
have been looking at you all this day, Tomass, and I
have seen how you look at me, with kindness, as you
did when I was *vep*—nothing more. It cannot be that
there should be anything more. But—but the Queen,
Tomass—she likes making love. She has had no official
husband for a dozen years because she prefers to
change her lovers frequently, and she expects much
from you even though you are a god. I think especially
because you are a god. We have many tales about the
gods, some of them serious ones preserved by the
elders, some of them amusing ones invented by the
people. One of the amusing ideas is that gods are as
sexy as fire-fish—that goddesses are pure essences of fe-
maleness, and male gods pure essences of maleness.
And yet—and yet I do not know if it is possible for a
god and a female Xuman to *make love*."

Saimo paused, then hung her head, and said softly,
"If it is important for your plans to make love with the
Queen, Tomass, well—I know you gods like to try
things out, to *experiment*. You experimented with me
before, when I was in the star-ship, in various ways.
Well, I still belong to you, Tomass, and now I am a female, in body just like the Queen, and—and I am
willing to help you in any way you wish, because I love
you and because I know that you plan only for the
good of Yelsai. If you will use my body so, master, I
will count that a great honor; I will not ask for love as
well."

I was touched, and also embarrassed. I put my hands

on Saimo's cheeks, and tilted her head, and kissed her lips.

"My dear child," I said, "thank you—thank you. But don't think I don't love you, Saimo—I do, in a way. Hell, I don't know how to put this—it's all mixed up inside me. But I'm not going to take you up on your offer. For one thing, I don't believe we could have satisfactory sex together—not you and I, not I and the Queen either. It's just an accident of biology—convergent evolution—that our two species happen to look so much alike that there can be a certain attraction . . . But all this stuff about Earthmen marrying gorgeous aliens is strictly for the birds—I mean, it's all nonsense. You, my dear—you're still very young. I hope you'll meet a nice Xuman boy one day . . . As for us—let's love each other, Saimo, like good friends." I laughed. "I hope I can make the Queen see things the same way."

"You do not want to sleep with her?" said Saimo, brightening.

"No," I said.

She cheered up at once. "Let us get ready for the feast," she said briskly.

But it was now only about sunset, and the feast was not scheduled for another hour or so. We had just washed, and Saimo had put on the new kilt the Palace servants had laid out, when there was a call of "Pui" at the door, and in came the two Counsellors, Psyl and Kanyo. Both were smiling pleasantly.

"We were thinking," said Psyl, "if you have time to spare, you might like to look over some parts of the Palace. The astronomy tower, for instance—that might interest a visitor from another world! And possibly young Saimo might like to see the training rooms of the young guardsmen . . ."

We accepted at once, and the two showed us the way. For some reason, I kept thinking of Psyl as "she" and Kanyo as "he," though of course both were grey-skinned with shortish blond hair and equally angular faces. Perhaps because Psyl was slightly shorter? I made a few tentative inquiries.

Kanyo laughed. "It is probably Psyl's managing manner; the female aspect is dominant in our world, you know, lord Tomass. But you are right in a sense, in our last phase, Psyl was a woman, and I was a man. As a matter of fact, we were married to each other."

I looked surprised. Psyl put in: "You must remember, we are Westerners. In the West Sector, there is no prejudice against inverts. And we have a higher proportion of them—almost one in twelve." She looked at Kanyo, and laughed softly. "When we first married, *I* was a man, and Kanyo was a *kynthi*."

"And she still dominated me even then—when *I* had the benefit of female sex," said Kanyo, smiling.

"You must be an exceptional couple," I said, interested.

"Not so much in the West," said Psyl. "I suppose the only really unusual thing about us is that we have kept in touch with each other after First Death. Most people manage to achieve the correct detachment, but there are some failures, and I'm afraid we are two of them. To stay together took some arranging, and I guess it's why we got kicked out of Khadan to a provincial post like this—it was behavior unbecoming in aged scholars."

"I suppose Khadan is the real capital of this planet," I said lightly.

They seemed to fall quiet. Kanyo said:

"It is the intellectual capital, certainly. Very austere, very academic. But it is not a *political* capital—we Elders have to be neutral in more senses than one. Do you have anything similar in your world, Tomass?"

"Well, there is Tycho," I said. "That is international territory; or, as we say in our language, *U.N.*"

They wanted to know at once about "U.N." Then Psyl said:

"So all your nations are United. That must be a great convenience."

"Er—yes," I said hurriedly. "It took a bit of doing, though. I was wondering why you hadn't managed to unite *your* planet. After all, you have had two million years, and you have cooperated fine as to the canals . . ."

"It is a matter of our deplorable psychology," said Kanyo with a wry smile. "It was proved a great while

ago—I won't say how many million years—that strife
and even violence are necessary to the happiness of
creatures with male and female sex, at least as the sexes
are arranged in the higher animals on Xuma. Possibly
on other worlds, with a different setup, there might be
no such tendency . . . anyway, at least it is certain that
violence is much less deadly among our lower animals.
Worm does not kill worm, nor fire-fish slaughter fire-
fish—"

"But the male fire-fish fight like demons," objected
Psyl.

"They pretend to. Well, yes, the basic aggression is
there, especially among the males, and it has to be
more serious in an intelligent species, where instincts do
not inhibit . . . With us Xumans, it is above all the
males who make *history*. History, in essence, means
murder; if you commit history on a large enough scale
you may call it *war*. We have had an amusing instance
of this lately, when the Queen's child Varan turned
male. At once the boy became much more interested in
swords and daggers, and now he spends much of his
time practicing martial skills among the young guardsmen. He also takes a great interest in history—I am his
teacher, so I know this—he questions me avidly. Varan
finds the history of Yelsai pretty boring—it is mainly a
list of small canals built and deserts reclaimed. But
Xarth! He is fairly wallowing in Xarthian history—all
those murders, battles, coups, massacres of Palace concubines, assassinations of Emperors . . ."

Saimo looked put out. "I thought the Prince was a
nice boy," she said.

"So he is," agreed Kanyo, "but he still wants to be a
warrior. This is merely normal male behavior. It is
probably because males do not bear children that they
seek to immortalize themselves by carving their names
on the world—especially on other people's bodies. But I
won't go into the philosophy of it now. The fact is, Tomass, in answer to your previous question, some half of
our race would find a condition of perfect unity and
stability—in other words, no *history*—much too boring.
Hence the division of our world into national states—

that gives scope for plenty of history. It is probably best so."

"But you elders—you could put an end to this if you wanted to," I said.

Kanyo spread his hands. "I do not know if there can be a meaningful answer to that question. For us to *want to*, we would have to be other than we are—so it is not true to say that *we* could want to abolish the national states. Anyway, we elders do not dispose of armies, if that is the kind of thing you mean."

Psyl said, "Saimo, my boy, wouldn't you like to see the young guardsmen now? The Prince will be with them, I think."

Saimo looked at me. "Go ahead," I said. "You can see, my lad, that we are managing the language fine now."

Kanyo took me to his own block, which was a kind of monastery within the Palace reserved for the royal gardeners and other Elders. The corridors were already the mayoralty of thon 2-3-0. I asked Kanyo what the glowing with those soft light-bowls which I had seen in power supply was for these lights.

"No power. It is simply a paint derived from certain luminous insects which we call *svitior*—star-worms. The bowls have to be repainted about once every six years, but the whole process is very cheap. We love cheap technology on Xuma. We have a principle about that, the principle of least disturbance. But how do you gods generate light?"

I explained the basic notions of electricity.

"Oh yes, we know the principle," said Kanyo. "It even has a few practical applications among us, certain little toys . . . not light, because it generates more heat than light, which violates the principle I mentioned. In any case this atom-sex is not a *source* of power, only a medium—and one which we have not needed to develop much."

I waited for Kanyo to question me about my collar radio and the aerial behind my head—but he did not. They had a curious lack of curiosity, these people.

Then we emerged onto the roof of the Astronomy

Tower. I found Kanyo's little telescopes very elegant, but I suppose not more advanced than that of the Earthly 19th or 20th Century. There were several wide-angle scopes for tracking the larger Ring fragments, and now that the sky was darkening he showed me how to use them.

"Your Vepan will be rising in the west there later this evening," he said. "Meanwhile we can look at anything else. Which star are you really from, may I ask?"

He had definitely said "star" (*sviti*), not "planet" (*xivayo*), although there were eight planets in the 82 Eri system. Planet 2 hung bright in the western sky above the sunset glow. I pointed to that.

"Couldn't we have come from there?" I asked.

I could not see his face in the dusk, but I guessed from his voice that he was smiling.

"Not unless you could live in boiling water," he said; "and all the rest of our planets are much too cold or— like our moon—are lumps of bare rock. No, Tomass, it is clear that you come from a planet of another star—I would say, a planet quite like ours but possibly with more water and less range of daily temperature. Am I right?"

"Right. Well—I guess it's no state secret. You *can* see our sun, as it happens, right now. Up there, on the edge of the Belt . . ."

Kanyo laughed. "That little one—the Toe of the Hamlor?"

"Yes," I said. "Yours looks equally unimpressive to us, I may say."

Kanyo brooded for a moment. "But it is right out of the galactic plane!"

"Why not? So is your sun to us."

"But," said Kanyo, "then your world is hardly any nearer to the galactic center than ours!"

"So what? What does that prove?"

"Oh, nothing," he said.

As we were walking back to the main palace block he said casually, "Tell me, Tomass—how long do you gods live?"

I saw no reason to lie. I told him. He uttered a sort of yelp.

"No longer than we! And yet you travel between stars! How?"

I explained about freezing.

"I admire your courage," he said.

Chapter Six

The Queen's feast took place on the great roof garden. The arrangements reminded me of what I had read in history books of Greco-Roman banquets—we had large two-person couches, a scattering of small tables, and a lot of servants—mostly well-grown children, a few young men—bringing round food and wine. These kids wore garlands of kaal and tula flowers—blue and yellow, the Yelsai national colors. Actually, there seemed to be flowers and vines everywhere. We were dining in a sort of clearing, with trellises and tree-sized tula stems all around us. If you did not glance down at the marble of the palace roof, you could fancy yourself in some jungle of ancient Earth.

The Queen gave me the place of honor beside her on her own couch; Saimo was placed nearby on a couch which she shared with Prince Varan. On the other side of us were Psyl and Kanyo—not reclining (this was improper for elders) but sitting up on a couple of chairs. Opposite us lay all twelve of those political Ladies, plus their various boyfriends.

It was a glorious evening, cool but not yet cold—all that water through and around Yelsai obviously made it

more temperate than the canal districts. Dinu, the little
asteroid-moon, shone brightly—that is, as brightly as it
could: it was waxing to full in its two-day orbit, but it
gave only about one-fifth of the light of full Moon on
Earth, and a damn sight less light, of course, than full
Earth on our Moon. To make up for its dimness, the
Ring Belt shimmered over a broad arch of the northern
sky, and several naked-eye rock fragments seemed to
crawl across the milky glow and the stars beyond. *Star-
worms*, Kanyo had told me, was a Xuman metaphor for
Ring fragments: it certainly seemed appropriate. And
there were real star-worms about, too: several of the
little insects were winking on the tula leaves. What with
the lights of heaven, and the worms, and several well-
shaded pink glow-globes, we had quite enough illumina-
tion on that roof to see each other's faces; but it was
also dim enough among those trellises to be weirdly romantic. In spite of the glamorous queen beside me, I
suddenly wished Sally were with us.

I soon realized that Queen Telesin was not inclined
to discuss politics during dinner. "Pleasure before
business," she said gleefully; "that is our Yelsai way."
She leaned against me, and made me drink from her
own wine cup—a great honor. I thought one or two of
the male guests opposite looked discontented at this,
but their Ladies beamed at us, and—well, encouraged
the Queen to fondle me. Several of them were fondling
their own "escorts"—if that was the right word. No, it
isn't—they were more like male concubines, kept men.
Some of the Ladies, I had learned, were married; but
they had left their husbands at home for this occasion—their partners were Palace guardsmen, with an
occasional "pervert" army captain thrown in.

During the dinner, we were entertained to a sort of
cabaret. There was a dance of handsome young boys,
then of more mature men, both wearing very brief costumes. When the second group came on, Telesin said:

"These are our best performers from the House of
the Spring Fire-fish. I hope you like them, Tomass.
They are young *kurar*, just turned from being *kynthi*. It
is our custom to keep them bound to state service for
one year after their change; after that, they are free to

leave the pleasure houses; but many of them prefer to stay. Most of these will, I imagine. Lovely perverts, aren't they?"

"I wouldn't know," I said.

She laughed. "Doubtless they don't interest you too much. All right, let's have some younger perverts still." She clapped her hands. "*Now* look, Tomass—these are from the same House."

That next dance was certainly something worth watching! The little kynthi from the House of the Spring Fire-fish could really move their bodies. They joined the male "perverts" in a ring-dance which Kanyo explained as having some deep symbolic significance— it was the Dance of Time, of Ending and Becoming— but his explanation was rather lost on me because I found it *becoming* in a different sense, or at least the girls' costumes were. What there was of them! For those kynthi-kids had on only a tiny patch of *fur* covering the place between their legs, and in the dim light of that roof garden I could certainly imagine that they were totally naked human girls with glowing red-brown skins, shapely bare breasts, and in fact shapely bare everything else . . . I felt the usual physical reaction taking place in me—and suddenly I lost confidence in what I had previously said to Saimo. Queen Telesin must be much older than these girls, but she didn't look it, or sound like it or *feel* like it, she felt like an Earth girl in her twenties, and—

—and the next moment I heard a rasping, metallic voice from my collar.

"Carson, come in please, come in please . . ."

Damn! I had left my bloody mentor-machine switched on with the volume up, and now *Riverhorse* was up over the hill and riding me again . . .

Well, I let them know I was still alive—and then things begun to get more businesslike. The dancing girls and boys were cleared away with the last food course, the male favorites opposite slunk out also, and we politicians were left sitting or reclining over our wine.

"And now," said Telesin pleasantly, grasping my shoulder, "normally we ladies reserve this time for amusing stories, but with tonight's mixed company I

David J. Lake

think not. Dear god from the stars, aren't you going to put a certain proposal to our city? Why not put it now?"

"All right," I said, sitting up straight. I patted my hip holster. "But first I want to demonstrate. Can you rig up some objects you don't mind losing? I want you to see what our weapons can do."

"We have already heard from credible witnesses—" began Telesin; but Prince Varan broke in:

"I would like to see, Mother. So would my friends." He nodded to the guards who were hovering in the background. "It may be very important to get a clear impression."

Telesin seemed a little shocked at her son's intervention, but some of the Ladies supported him, so she shrugged, and I got my demonstration. On the parapet of that roof I annihilated a crate of assorted garden rubbish and an old stone baluster; I showed Varan the different power settings; and then we returned to our seats.

"And you have many more such weapons up there?" said young Varan, pointing to the bright star that was now sweeping up from the western horizon.

"Hundreds," I said, "and some with much bigger beams."

"Some big enough to destroy a city in a few seconds?" said Kanyo quietly.

"Yes," I admitted.

"From there," he said, pointing to the sky. It did not sound like a question.

"Yes, from there," I agreed. "It's not easy to bring the biggest ones down to the surface, but in any case we don't need to, they are more effective where they now are. Any city that defies us we can wipe out from space: the present orbit brings us sufficiently over any city between the Equator and 45 degrees north or south—I mean, halfway to the poles—and of course we could vary the orbit if necessary . . ."

"So you have us entirely at your mercy," said Psyl.

"I wish you wouldn't put it like that," I said. "We are not monsters from outer space! I *like* you people. I love Yelsai—I've seen nothing like it in my life, it's marvellous, and I also like what I've heard about some other cities of your planet—the West Sector, for instance. Psyl, Kanyo, and you, Queen Telesin, Prince Varan—I would like to be your friend." I had drunk just the right amount of that noble golden wine to feel sincerely emotional. "I'm your *friend*," I repeated; "all intelligent life should stick together, for that matter. All we—er, gods—all we want from you is a little mutual aid. You need help against Xarth—we can supply it. Telesin, my sweet—we can hand you the Empire of Xarth on a platter—make you the greatest Empress that Xuma has ever seen."

"And in return?" said Kanyo.

"In return—just a place in the sun," I said. "I mean—in *your* sun. 'Fact is, our race needs more living room: there are certain—er—difficulties on our home planet. Now, you could cede us a city or two, and not even notice it."

"But I have only one city," said Telesin, bewildered.

"Now, yes. But when we have made you *Empress of all Xuma*?"

There was a sudden silence. Then Telesin burst out into wild musical laughter—laughter like an explosion of glockenspiel. When she had recovered, she said, "Forgive me, god Tomass. But surely you are joking! How could I be Empress of all Xuma?"

"We could kill any man who resisted your claim."

She looked at me now seriously. "But I *have* no claim. I have been chosen Queen by the people of Yelsai, not by the people of the East or the West or Xarth. And even if the others suddenly decided to make me a world Empress—why, I would refuse. I am a Yelsai woman, I was a farm girl on the East Canal before I was chosen for this palace—no, I wouldn't do it! I love being Queen of Yelsai, and you want to take all this away from me! Oh, Tomass, please *no!*"

"But you wouldn't lose anything; you would simply gain the whole world as well."

"Excuse my rudeness," said Kanyo suddenly, "but you are talking nonsense, Tomass. The Queen is right—a person who gains the whole world loses his own individuality. As our philosophers showed long ago, infinity and zero are equivalent. Tomass, if you are going to be a tempter, at least please try to make your bait a desirable one."

I heard a hiss from my collar. It was Mannheim. "Carson, translations are overdue. Can't you tell us how the negotiations are going?"

"Er—they seem a bit skeptical, skipper. They're not sure they want to conquer the whole world, anyway."

"Make it the Central and East Sectors then," said Mannheim, "and tell them to quit stalling. If they don't like the deal, we can always take our offer elsewhere. Say, that might not be a bad idea anyway. That Emperor of Xarth, now—he sounds as though we could do business with *him*, all right."

"I advise against that," I said hastily. "From my information, he is an unbalanced personality, and a sexual pervert. Xarth is not a stable polity—they might try to double-cross us. Look, let me handle this, will you? If they refuse outright, we can always think again."

I turned to the Xumans. "Look, I like you people—" I began; but Telesin cut me off.

"What is all this *conquering* about, anyway? Tomass, how many of you gods are there up in that thing? Eight dozen, is it? We can easily find houses for that number of people even in this one city, and give you country houses too on any of our canals—big beautiful houses. We would be most honored if you would become our guests—our permanent guests."

"Thank you," I said, "but it's not as easy as that. There are only a hundred of us in our present starship, but there are others back on our home world who are also looking for a better place to live. They too want living room. And then there will be children. We need a good deal of room to expand into—several cities all to ourselves, at least."

"There is something very badly wrong here," said Psyl. "*Why* do you people need more living room? What *has* gone wrong with your planet? Is it as much as went wrong with *our* planet two-and-a-half million years ago, and if so, whose fault is it? I—"

"Psyl, stop it!" said Kanyo sharply. "There are questions Tomass may not wish to answer, and some that we had better not ask."

In spite of the evening chill, I was sweating. "Look," I said, "please, *please* agree to go along with our plan at least to some extent. If you don't—"

"You will offer your weapons to Xarth," said Prince Varan. He was sitting upright, tense and grim, one hand firm on Saimo's shoulder. "Yes, my young friend here heard all that you said into that thing, Tomass— and my friend understands your language, don't forget."

"Well, now you've got it straight," I said. "Look, I hate this situation myself, and I'd like to help you out of it any way I know, but the only way is to play along. Play for time: agree to use our help, first against Xarth—then we'll see what can be done."

"Please do as Tomass says," put in Saimo suddenly. "He is good, very good—but not all gods are good." She checked herself, abashed at her own boldness.

One of the Ladies opposite suddenly spoke up. "We all think it would be wise to use the god-weapons against Xarth," she said. "All the indications are that the Emperor is planning a war of conquest against us this very winter. Even with the aid of Tlanash, we might not be able to hold out—and then Yelsai would go the way of Nakaan." She shuddered. "In ordinary circumstances, we might have to say 'it is the wind of Time,' and suffer that. But these are not ordinary circumstances! Retumon has broken sacred custom, by violating the hudaan—therefore it would not be wrong for us to break custom too. That is our thought, O Queen."

"It is what I advise also," said Kanyo. "Time! Yes, we must go with it a little differently now—go with it, and play for it. Tomass, I hope Saimo is right—that there are many good persons among your crew."

"It might be easier if there were not," said Psyl bitterly. "Queen Telesin, we advise that you accept the proposal for war against Xarth, and that you allow the sky folk to land many more of their people. No—*allow* is not the word, but if they wish to land, make no opposition. Tomass," she said earnestly, turning to me, "are you really on our side?"

"Yes," I said.

"Then, if your leader up there proposes names of people to land at once, try to get him to include the woman Sally and the man Dave and . . ." She rattled off a string of names: they included all my particular friends, who were also people who had been nice to Saimo during the past months.

"I see you have been conferring," I said, glancing at Saimo. "Why do you want those to land?"

"Because I think they will be more amiable," said Psyl.

"Makes sense," I said, and looked at the Queen. Telesin nodded sideways, which meant "yes."

"Tell your Emperor just that, Tomass," she said, "but ask him not to land anybody till tomorrow morning. It is late, and we of Yelsai like to sleep."

"Sure," I said, and got on to Mannheim at once. He was grudgingly pleased with my success, and he agreed to the proposals for a landing party. I at once felt happy. It would be great to have Sally down here!

As I finished speaking to Mannheim, the *Riverhorse*, that little crawling star-worm, crawled into the black gap of the planet's shadow, and vanished as though swallowed by some cosmic predator. I turned the volume of my radio right down; and then I noticed that the two elders were no longer with us. The Ladies, too, were making obvious preparations to depart.

"Tomass, that was exhausting," said Telesin, leaning her lithe warm body against me and caressing my shoulder; "and now we both deserve some reward for finishing all that business. Will you come and have a little drink in my private apartments? Varan will take care of your little friend."

And then, I'm afraid, I said: "Can do!"

The Queen's apartment—hell, let's be frank, bedroom—it was decorated mainly in dark red, with red-shaded glow-bowls. The light and the decor blended very well with the color of her skin.

She was soon showing me a lot of her skin.

There was nobody else in the room when we entered it, but there was wine on a table and a couple of glasses. The wine was not yellow, but blue—in that light a very dark blue.

"It is *lyl dlu*—Water of Dreams," said Telesin. "Let your machine sip a little of it, Tomass. It does us no harm, but since you are a god ..."

But my Taster passed that Water of Dreams: it was good old ethyl, 18%, with a trace of a mild sedative.

"If you drink too much, you will sleep," she said, smiling, "but a little is very nice." She poured, and we drank. It was a marvellous wine, sweet but not too sweet, with a tang like cold fire. We drank off that first glass pretty fast. Then she said:

"I am hot, Tomass. Please, will you help me off with this gown?"

I did. Now she was wearing nothing but a little black cloth about her loins—a cloth the color of her hair, and not much wider than a belt. But she still had on her bracelets and her jewel-pendant crown. Nothing on her feet but a couple of gold anklets.

"Let me be your wine-slave-girl," she said, kneeling before me, and pouring again. "Do you know, Tomass, in Xarth that crazy Emperor has girls as his servants? Normal girls as well as kynthi. They pour his wine, and—"

"And what?" I said, leaning towards her and laughing.

"Oh, I am too modest to say," she said, fluttering her eyelashes. "May I pour you some more, my master? Another will not harm you."

"Yes ..." I said, taking the glass from her slim red fingers.

"Let me make you more comfortable," she said, after a while.

Well, she helped me off with my collar radio, and then with my holster, which she laid carefully on the table.

I have to admit that by now I was getting pretty excited. At the back of my mind was a faint sense of *déjà vu*. Till this expedition, in my lifetime humans had had hardly any chance to mingle with people of other races—especially not sexually. But there had been one time in Tycho when I had met a Chink girl. It had not gone as far as any kind of affair—I had realized at once that if we even held hands I'd never get space clearance again, and she was almost certainly a spy for her side, too. But at that U.N. cocktail party we had met, and talked, and there had been a definite feeling . . . I had the same sort of feeling now. Excitement at my lady's strange beauty, perhaps even a little fear of her strangeness, and a strong desire to dare all the barriers between us, all the differences.

I guess Telesin felt it too, the same thing about me.

"O my beautiful god Tomass," she breathed, "you are so strange, with your nipples like a woman" (she had my shirt partly undone now, and knew whereof she spoke), "your pale skin like an Elder, your grey eyes, your brown hair. Your strength—your godly strength! You are so strong—stronger than any boy of my people, stronger even than any kurar. The tale is true, I think —male gods are like fire-fish, pure male and only male . ₃ ."

"You are so right," I said, laughing and playing with her exquisitely-arranged hair, ruffling it. "I *am* only male, Telesin, I've never been a female in my life, and I never will be one."

"Truly?" she said, astonished, checking her caresses.

"Truly. We Earth humans are born sexed—we are *either* males or females forever, never *both*. I am thirty years old—'bout thirty-seven by your reckoning—and I've been a boy all that time, my sweet, and I always will be. I'm so so glad I'll never *be* a girl—I *like* girls too much for that. Here—c'm 'ere—lemme show you . . ."

"O my glorious god!" she breathed, almost choking with emotion, her strange eyes wide.

Then she was naked and I was naked, and we were on the great royal bed. We tussled a little at first—a laughing misunderstanding, for she was used to getting on top as a matter of royal protocol, but when she saw what I wanted to do, she laughed again, and let me throw her on her back.

I guess somebody should put up a plaque in that room—a tasteful memorial on the wall, or standing free on four metal legs. HERE IN JULY 2143 / FIRST

MONTH 9-9-2-0-8-5 TOMASS CARSON, EARTH-MAN, AND TELESIN OF YELSAI, XUMAN *KUN*, FIRST PROVED THAT—but I'm not sure how the inscription should end. LOVE WILL FIND A WAY, perhaps; followed by WE CAME, IN PEACE FOR ALL MAN- AND XUMAN-KIND. The fact is that though human and Xuman equipment are far from identical, a human male *can* get into a Xuman female.

I found Telesin gorgeous, delightful, and I managed. When it was over, and we had come apart, she sighed.

"Is that all?" she said.

Then I discovered how very much more the Xuman male does. You know, there are some Earth creatures—various insects, for example—that have to be coupled for hours when they are mating. It does not take the Xumans quite that long, but by our standards it is *long*. Also, the Xuman male thing is tooled to fit exactly all over that pretty disc-like slot, whereas I—ah, what the hell. I had had a good time—well, a goodish time—but Telesin was not satisfied. Not *satisfied*! That was the first time I had heard *that* complaint from any girl I had gone with; I thought myself a pretty adequate stud . . .

"Let's try again, darling," said Telesin. "But first, maybe you'd like a drink . . .?"

I did. In fact, I wanted several, and she gave me what I wanted. Then she began to caress me, in all sorts of places. I guess I was pretty drunk, and a bit blurry with that Water-of-Dreams drug, and yet we kept up a conversation. It sort of wandered from human-type sex to human-type life in general. I told her about the Moon.

"You mean you have to live *under glass domes*? Outside the domes there is *no air*? Heart of Being, Tomass, how could your planet get so terrible?"

"It's not our planet," I said thickly. "It's only our *moon*, a hunk of rock like your moon, only bigger. We messed up our own planet long ago—fought wars over it, with shit-awful weapons—not lasers—well, yes, lasers too. Only a few wild people live there now. World War Three was mainly atomics, and World War Four was mainly germs. My father died on an expedi-

tion to Earth—caught an artificial virus from one of
the savages. If there's a World War Five it will be on
the Moon itself, and I don't think anybody will survive.
That's why we're here, Queenie—to find a place to hide
if the Chinks and the Russky cities start firing at our
cities. The Chinks and the Russkies are sending out
ships, too—the Chinks to 70 Ophiuchi, the Russ to
Sigma Draconis. And may the best man win," I said,
spilling my wine over the bed. "Come here, sweetie,
gimme a kiss . . ."

"Tomass, you have drunk too much," said Telesin
severely. "It makes a male not able—"

"Not able? 'Course I'm able! Just you come here, my
poppet, and see if I don't make you lay an egg in nine
months time—"

"Lay an *egg*! Tomass, have you gone out of your
mind? We Xumans do not lay eggs! Do human females
lay eggs?"

"Forget about eggs. Jus' a silly lit'ry reference. Just
come here, Telsy, and gimme a nice, nice kiss—"

I don't know what she would have done if we had
been left to our own devices; perhaps she would have
kissed me, and humored me until I fell into a deep
drugged and drunken sleep. But the question can only
have meaning in one of those parallel universes the SF
writers talk about, because we were not left to our own
devices.

As I was pawing Telesin, the great door which led
onto the roof garden was flung open, with a dreadful
sound of splintering, and a half-dozen red-skinned
kilted warriors burst into the room, their swords drawn.

One of the warriors had conical nippled breasts
above her kilt. Her leather straps bore the three gold
stars of a *hazyo* (colonel), she carried a sword—and
wore a silver skull-mask. As Telesin and I lay on the
bed, naked and paralyzed with shock, she pointed her
sword at us.

"*Patu lua*," she barked. "Take her!"

Telesin screamed. "Tomass, it is the Xarthians!"

I stumbled groggily to my feet at the side of the bed.
I wanted to dive for my laser, but the Xarthians were
already upon us. Three of the male warriors grabbed

Telesin, and began pulling her towards the doorway. Another two got between me and my laser, and raised their swords. I thought I was done for.

The woman colonel suddenly yelled.

"Bring that one too, the freak! It may be important. Don't kill it!"

The next moment, they had lowered their swords and grabbed me. One pulled me by a wrist, the other got behind me and prodded my naked back with his sword. They were driving me to the door, through which the others had now hustled Telesin.

I was sobering and shedding my sleepiness rapidly. I noticed that they were ignoring my gear—the pack and collar radio and laser. I wondered what that signified.

Then we were out on the roof garden—and I heard sounds of a battle raging. Among the trellises, the trunks and leaves of tula, there was sword play going on; red man was striking at red man, and some were falling. The light of the glow-globes and the small moon gleamed off the clashing steel—but I was in no mood to appreciate the beauty of the scene. The cold air made me catch my breath—it also cleared my wits sufficiently for me to realize that the Xarthians were outnumbered, and more Yelsai guardsmen were racing up. So: the city had not fallen to invaders, this was more like a raid; but how . . . ?

Telesin and I were being driven by the raiders to the edge of the roof—and there I saw in the moonlight a *gola*, a balloon-ship, obviously grappled to the parapet and straining in the constant east wind. The balloon was bobbing up and down, and the boat-shaped car was almost level with the parapet. In a few moments our captors would have us over the wall, into their craft, and then—

Telesin turned her lovely face to me, as she fought with the men who held her.

"Tomass," she cried, "do not let them take me away! They are taking me to their Emperor, to be his slave, to dismay our people!"

What could I do? In my position of course any real hero would have burst from his captors, and, exerting the force of his Earthly, super-Xuman muscles, would have brained all the tormentors of his beautiful alien Queen with a few blows of his bare fists, and captured their flying craft single-handed. I, however, not being a hero, and being also tired and drunk and naked, could do nothing against the swords that were raised against us. I stumbled forward.

"We'd better go quietly, I think," I said. "Maybe Mannheim can negotiate . . ."

But in the next instant the whole situation was transformed. One moment the balloon was there—the next moment it wasn't. I stared stupidly at the space beyond the parapet: over the grappling hooks a piece of fabric like a gigantic bat was flapping upwards, revealing the peaceful stars. From below, out of sight, I could hear dwindling shrieks.

And on the roof, a few paces behind us, a young red-skinned warrior burst out of the cover of the vegetation. I recognized Prince Varan: he was holding a small tube in his hands. He shouted, in a great voice:

"Surrender, Xarthians, or you are all dead!"

The woman colonel leapt to Telesin's side, and menaced her with her sword. She was obviously about to try the hostage trick, but she did not get out even one word of her threat. In the next second, she had simply ceased to exist. Well, her masked and helmeted head clattered to the roof along with her sword, mixing with the gruesome remains of the lower half of her body. And with another couple of hand movements Varan eliminated all the rest of the Queen's immediate captors, handling the laser with cool skill and economy of effort. He was a natural gunman, that boy.

The other Xarthians had had enough. The warriors who were holding me threw down their swords, and so did the two or three others who had been still battling the Yelsai guards further down the roof.

A moment later, Saimo emerged from the shrubbery and stood beside Varan. She was wearing a high-collared lady's gown.

Telesin, though she was stark naked, had quite regained her composure. She smiled graciously at Varan.

"Well done, my child," she said. "That was intelligent of you. Of course, the Xarthians must have

106

planned this outrage long before the landing of To-mass—their balloon-ship must have been launched from one of the Eastern canals. If only Tomass had got to his magic weapon in time, he might have spared you the trouble. Now, Varan, you had better hand the god back his weapon, there's a good boy."

"God? What *god*?" said Varan, with a touch of scorn which I thought was really uncalled for. "I see here only a foreigner, a creature of an alien race who was not even able to protect his mistress, my mother, when he had the advantage of weapons. I will keep this—this death-dispenser, for the good of my country, Yelsai—"

"Varan!" cried Telesin, "that is no way for a boy to talk—a *male*! To a *woman*, your mother and your Queen!"

Varan looked rebellious, but I said:

"Look, Prince, I think I know how you feel, but I really would advise you to put that thing down—put it away in a safe place, at least. You can't do much for Yelsai with *one* laser of that size—our guys will be landing tomorrow with *dozens*. And we've got really big ones in orbit. So . . .?"

Varan really was intelligent. He thought for a second, then laid down the blaster on a little table that had survived the battle.

"You are right. In any case, it is not an honorable weapon." He paused, and looked his mother straight in the eyes. "From now on, I shall *take charge* of the guards of this palace personally—and make sure that they are kept alert, and fully efficient in swordsmanship. It is true that *gola* was disguised as an Eastern trader, but that is not sufficient excuse. What happened tonight should never have been allowed to happen. I will see that it does not happen again."

"Since when do you have authority—" began Telesin.

"Since I rescued you, Mother," said Varan. "Have I not proved my authority? Your guards are *my* guards now: this palace is in my hands, and the hands of my men. I do not wish to lead a rebellion, but—there should be some changes in Yelsai, I think. You and your Ladies can make them official. For one thing, men

107

must be given some power and respect. A city of women will not stand against Xarth!"

"The boy's right," I said.

"And another change," said Varan, "must be in the treatment of *kynthi*. They too are people, and deserve the respect of people! Anyone who insults or tries to harm or enslave my friend Saimo will have to reckon with me. It was she who drew my attention to what was happening this night, and therefore it was she, ultimately, who saved our Queen."

The Yelsai guards murmured respectfully. I stared at Saimo.

"She?" I said—and then I noticed: tiny nipples were showing on Saimo's budding breasts.

"Yes, she," said Varan. "She, my friend, my love. My princess."

Saimo blushed. "Forgive me, Tomass, but I know now that you were right, you are not for me, you are too high . . ."

I shivered, and hiccuped. "Too damn' right you are, Angel—I'm a good deal too high. Even now . . ."

Telesin laid her arm on my goose-fleshed shoulder. "Come, Tomass, let me put you to bed," she said soothingly.

Chapter Seven

I woke up cold and lonely and feeling sorry for myself. I was in my own room in the palace, and the sun was coming in at the window shutters in thin but dazzling beams that hurt my eyes. Boy, did I have a hangover!

Saimo's bed was empty, and obviously had not been slept in. I was alone.

I groaned, recalling the previous evening. Gradually, most of it came back—including my bedroom patter to Telesin. I had been telling her about our sexes, and about life on the Moon. How much had I said about that? I couldn't be quite sure. Surely I hadn't mentioned the Russians and the Chinks? I would have had to be insane to do that! No, surely I hadn't mentioned them . . .

I was feeling just a fraction better, when someone knocked at the door.

This should have told me something, but it didn't—you see, I still wasn't very bright. I said *"Xi inu,"* which in Xuman is more or less "Come in"—and then she came in.

"Hi there, Tommy," she said. "Wish I'd had as much sleep as that last night."

She was Sally.

She was wearing uniform black slacks and blouse, which set off her fair skin and blonde hair very nicely. In fact, she looked marvellous. I threw off my sleeping quilts.

"Sal!" I gasped, "what—"

She gave a wolf whistle. "What a marvellous sight, Tom!"

"Oh—oh yes," I said, covering up again. In my excitement I'd forgotten I wasn't wearing a thing under the bedclothes.

"Don't mind me," said Sally, plumping herself down on the bed, and giving me a hug and kiss. "I've seen as much before, darling, only not quite enough lately. Say, what've you been up to in these heathen parts? Don't tell me, I can guess—I've seen some of the local birds, and knowing my Tom Carson—"

"Cut it out," I groaned. "Look, Sal, what's been happening this morning?"

"Program nominal," she smiled. "We put down in four landers at the—the airport, just after local sunrise. Fourteen of us altogether, including Dave and Rosa and Jack Willis, but also some of Mannheim's gang. We thought you'd be there to meet us, but no—the head of the welcoming party told us you'd had a heavy night and were sleeping it off. He was a young kid, name of Varan, and he had Saimo with him as interpreter. Say, Saimo's turned into quite a fetching girl, hasn't she? She was wearing one of those Old-Cretan-type gowns—bare top in front—all very chic. She told me she slept with you on your first night down, by the way."

"It wasn't at all what you think," I protested. "Cut out the wise-cracks—sex between Xumans and humans is just no go."

"Oh, so you *have* tried the experiment? You must give me the details later. I certainly don't imagine Xuman boys would be very *fitting* mates for Earth girls. Pity," she sighed. "I think some of Prince Varan's young guardsmen are very, very handsome. They seem interested, too—several of them were giving me and Rosa the glad eye at the airport, and that's pretty good

going for six-thirty in the morning. They were calling
us 'goddesses,' according to Saimo! Varan seemed less
impressed, though. At first he took me for an elder!"

"Pale skin, pale hair—that figures. Look, d'you mind
if I get up?"

"Go right ahead." She laughed. "I'd soap your back,
my love, if I knew what to soap with."

"Yeah, well, it's kind of primitive," I said, staggering
into the wash corner. Wincing, I splashed myself with
cold water and rubbed on the soft goo which is the
Xuman soap. "See what I mean? Not like the hot show-
ers in the *Horse*, Sal."

She gave me a slow smile. "I love it, Tom."

"Eh?"

"I said, I love it, this planet, this city. Tom, these
people—they're living the way we humans should have
lived—the way our forefathers maybe *did* live on old
Earth hundreds of years ago. Oh, not in details, I
guess—here the details are *better* . . ."

"It's not perfect," I said, yelping as I washed off the
'soap.' "You know they've got state prostitution? That's
what the young girls do for their *National Service*."

"I know. That's just one little aberration—you can
see how it might arise, what with the surplus of men,
two to a wife and all that. Anyway, it's going to be
stopped, I believe. And, Tom, this place is so *beautiful*!
It's the kind of place I dreamed of when I was working
at Lunaris zoo among those caged dogs and horses. It's
like coming home. I'm getting used to the gravity, and I
think I can adapt to cold water! At least, there's *natural
air to breathe*."

"Not all Xuma is as nice as Yelsai," I grunted.
"Have you heard about Xarth?"

"Yes—and there's more yet which *you* haven't heard.
Looks like we're going into action quicker than we expected. You may not know it, but there's a war on,
Tommy. Varan says balloon-raiders from Xarth have
been hitting the West Canal all along its length in the
early hours this morning, and the main army came over
the frontier an hour before dawn. They have simultaneously attacked south along the next canal, thirty

degrees east of here; that's into the territory of our allied city, Tla something."

"Tlanash."

"Right. Y'know, there's something damn familiar about all this—you'd think that Xarth Emperor had been reading up Earth history. Sounds like a 20th-Century blitzkrieg, Nazi style. Varan has questioned the prisoners he took last night in the raid on this palace, and it seems they bought up a fleet of East Sector trading balloons and launched them from the canal on the Tlanash front. This palace was a "target of opportunity," you might say—they can't be sure exactly where they're going to land up. The balloon troops are not really an air force in the Earthly sense—more like parachutists. But I know one thing."

"What?"

"I'm damn glad we joined this side, Tommy. Whatever I hear about that Xarthian Emperor gives me the shivers. He has the real conquistador instinct. If he had a *real* air force—if he had *us*—Yelsai and Tlanash would have been lasered out of existence already. Manheim, by the way, was calmly proposing to wipe out a city or two with his big guns from orbit just before we took off. He thought the two minor cities of Xarth might serve as a demonstration—what are they called? Hiroshima and Nagasaki?"

"Hiraxa and Nakaan."

"Yes. Well, luckily the majority of us troops were against that. So is Prince Varan. He says Hira and Naka are subject cities anyway, and if we hit the Xarthians just enough to show that they can't win, both cities will rise against their masters, and the war will be practically over. I like that boy. He has exactly the right ideas. I'm glad he is to be C-in-C of our allies."

"What? Since when?"

"Since dawn today. The Yelsai government—twelve ladies and the Queen—held an emergency session and appointed him. It's been a busy night for all of us, it seems—I don't know about you. We space folk had to get into those landers in the early hours, of course—we've been keeping this area's time, you remember. Lucky Tommy, to get in your solid eight hours . . ."

I groaned. "If only you knew," I said.

Someone had left all my gear neatly arranged by my bed, so I now dressed, and buckled on my laser. I was going to leave the radio, when Sally said:

"Better take that, too. Sure, you don't need it to keep in touch with the *Horse*—Belmondo's doing that—but I've been briefed to watch out for technological spying by the locals."

"Oh yeah? Well, why don't *you* wear the damn thing for a change."

"O.K.," said Sally, and put on the collar-plus-antenna.

Outside, we found a couple of young guardsmen. They smiled at Sally, gave us both that two-handed salute, and then led us to a large chamber in the heart of the palace. Here we found a conference in session—Varan and Saimo on a pair of ornate chairs—well, call them thrones—flanked by a lot of guardsmen. Facing them on a row of plainer chairs were black-uniformed Earthfolk—First Officer Belmondo, Dave Weiser, Rosa Meyer, and three other crew members—all males—whom I knew to be members of Mannheim's gang. Every one of our people was wearing a laser, even gentle little Rosa who I knew hated the things, and Belmondo was wearing a radio as well.

I greeted Belmondo officially, and Dave and Rosa more cordially. Rosa, besides being a hell of a good botanist, was Dave's girl, dark-haired like him, and pretty—unlike him.

"Great to see you, Tom," said Rosa, with her usual understated but really warm smile. "Come and join the briefing. I guess you can help with the translations."

"Briefing?"

"Sure," said Dave, grinning darkly under his thick mobile eyebrows. "There's a war on, haven't you heard? This is Air Force headquarters now. We are about to fly a mission in support of the troops. B.B. here is raring to go, but the Prince is trying to explain via Angel which redskins are bad redskins."

"Have you seen the Queen?" I asked.

"Yes," said Rosa. "Quite a beauty, isn't she? She was here earlier, but then she left us. I think she said she

113

had to rest, and she had every confidence in Varan's judgment of military matters."

"Things *have* changed," I said, looking at the Xumans. "Not a single *kun* woman in sight!"

Varan now addressed me. "Will you explain to your people," he said, "that I want them to take their fliers up the West Canal and destroy the advancing Xarthians. They can tell them by their skull-masks, but they'll have to fly low to distinguish those. For that matter, Tomass, it would be best if I were there. Our main army is still holding them; they're in close contact. I must order them to retreat slightly." He paused, looking at me doubtfully. "Could you possibly fly me to the front yourself, and land me behind our lines?"

I passed my hand over my head. "I'm not feeling too good, but I guess I could—"

"I'll give you some pills," said Sally, gripping my arm and laughing. "When I heard they had such fine wines, I included some of that sort in my medi-pack."

"O.K. then," said Belmondo, "let's go, troops."

Yelsai airport that morning looked transformed. The trading balloons had all vanished, and in their places four astro-landers of various sizes were drawn up neatly before the paved area and the buildings. Some of our guys were cruising about in an S/V—surface vehicle: for which, in this case, read "light tank." They clattered over the flagstones and tore bruised strips in the blue-green grass as though they were really achieving something. They had the pressure dome down in this benign atmosphere, and some clown was standing erect fingering the grip of the laser-cannon as though he would like to try shooting up hostile natives. There were a couple of tall fair-skinned Earth girls standing before the main building admiring the guys in the S/V, and being themselves admired by a small crowd of red-skinned Xumans, mostly naked kids and kilted young men.

During the ride to the airport I had learnt what arrangements our landing force had made. Belmondo had insisted that Varan hand over one of the airport buildings—the big central one—as expedition HQ, and this was now christened "the Fort." I might have guessed it:

114

Belmondo and Mannheim thought pretty well alike, and they did not trust our allies. Already one little patch of Xuma was conquered territory.

"We've gotta keep our weapons and equipment safe," Belmondo had said. "And the girls. I don't like the way the red boys look at them. As long as I'm in command, they'll sleep in the Fort—nowhere else."

When I climbed into my little flier with Varan, I was feeling slightly sick—and that wasn't due to my hangover, which Sally's pills had pretty well cured.

Varan was silent at first as we flew along the blue-green line of the West Canal. He was of course fascinated by his first view of his own world from such a height and drifting by at such a speed (the golas usually travel low, and always slow). But after he had registered the scene, he turned to me and said abruptly:

"Tomass—"

"What?"

"I'm sorry I was rude to you last night. Saimo says you are a good man."

"Thanks. Look, you had every right to be rude. I was drunk, and pretty useless. I'll be more careful in future. By the way, Prince, I like the way you are handling things—you and your young guardsmen. Yelsai is a fine city, but you're right, some changes are necessary. Men's Liberation, for instance."

"True," said Varan, "but I think that will not be a great problem. I have a solid following now among the young guards, and the women will soon find that they cannot do without us. But there are much worse things that we are facing. Tomass, have you ever been invaded—your people, I mean? Your country?"

"Well, no. But I've heard how it feels like. My grandfather was English—he was one of the last people to get away from Britain before World War IV. Britain was then a colony of the Russians. Wow! Maybe that's something I should not have said."

Varan grinned, but grimly. "It is too late to hide such matters, Tomass. The Queen has told me what you told her about the Russians and the Chinkians. I know very well now that you folk from the Toe of the Hamlor are not gods, and some of you are not much

115

better than Retumon of Xarth. But some of you *are*
better. You are very *like* us—on average, neither better
nor worse. Some of you I like—the same ones that
Saimo said she liked. But this Belmondo—is he your
friend?"

"No . . ." And I told him what I thought of
Mannheim, too, and quite a few others of our crew.

Varan said quietly: "One day, Tomass, you will have
to make up your mind."

"Eh?"

"As to whose side you are on. Today there is no
great problem. Today we are all on the same side, killing Xarthians. But I think this war will not last very
long, and then—then there may be other wars. I hope
that then we two will be on the same side."

I was silent. A moment or two later, we had reached
our destination.

Well, the battles that day were a pushover. I landed
Varan in a meadow of thon 2-4-2, just behind the Yelsai battle line, and he rushed out and found the Yelsai
woman-general and issued the necessary orders to her
troops. All along that three-mile battlefront of fields
and farms the Yelsaians suddenly ran away, and the
skull-masked Xarthians yelled with ferocious joy and
came streaming after them. We had timed it just right.
I was talking the landers down, and seconds later the
four of them came swooping in from the east, lasers
blazing. Talk about rolling up a flank! It was more like
hosing away a line of red ants. In a couple of minutes,
there simply *wasn't* a Xarthian army on that front.

Then the landers wheeled and flew away southeast
towards Tlanash.

"There should not be any problem about our Tlanash
allies," said Varan, as he climbed back into my plane.
"They are in full flight already—real rout. The Emperor launched his main attack against them, and broke
them. But for you 'gods,' Tlanash itself would soon be
under siege, and then it would have been Yelsai's turn.
So, Tomass, we really have a good deal to be grateful
to you for. I think you have saved our city—at least,
from the Xarthians."

I got the implication of his last remark. As we took off again, I said:

"Mannheim doesn't want Yelsai. He wants those lush cities in the East."

"Tomass," said the young prince, "I am not a fool—and I think you are not, either. Does it matter which city you mainly occupy—when you can take any city by merely asking for it?"

I had no answer to that. "Believe me," I said, "I hate what's happening. But what's the alternative? For me, I mean?"

"This," said Varan, leaning forward in his seat. "You can become one of us."

"Eh?"

"You can become citizens, you and your good friends—citizens of Yelsai, or of any other friendly city if you prefer. It does not matter about your peculiar sexes, now that we are breaking down the prejudice against perverts. It will not matter even if you breed and multiply, within reason—you will simply be two more Xuman sex groups, along with kurar and kynthi. The big thing, the important thing, is to stop thinking of 'you against us,' or 'us against you.' What my mother said last night is quite true, Tomass—you can easily live among us with no question of domination, neither domination of you by us or us by you. Why can't we just be friends?"

It all seemed so simple, put like that. Then I remembered Mannheim and the laser cannon on *Riverhorse*; and I felt sick.

"Varan, it would come to shooting, and I would have to shoot either you or my friends, and anyway Mannheim's bunch are sure to win, so what can I do?"

"I am not asking you to shoot your *friends*," he said, "not even to shoot at the star-folk you dislike. I say again, Tomass, I am not a fool: I do not intend to battle against hopeless odds. But sometimes there is room for—let us say, little maneuvers." He paused, watching the way I handled the controls. Then he went on, apparently changing the subject:

"Tomass, can you show me how to do that?"

"What?"

"Fly this machine."

I laughed. "Well, why not? There's an automatic override if you do something foolish. It's only the landing that's really tricky."

"What happens if you make a bad mistake?"

"Then there's the ejector. If the override fails, or if you've switched it off, it throws you clear of the plane with a parachute to bring you down softly."

"But the flier itself is destroyed?"

"Yes." I considered. "But it won't come to that; I've given other guys lessons before, on Old Mars. O.K., come here. This is what you do. . . ."

Well, I gave him a brief lesson. Not only was that boy a natural born gunman, he was a natural born flier. Before we reached Yelsai he was confident about flying the lander straight, turning, going up or down, levelling and switching from manual to auto and back.

As I took over again for the landing, Varan was eyeing the small laser cannon built into the ship's nose.

"I suppose that is also simple to operate?" he said.

I looked at him in alarm. If I taught him *that*, there'd be only one word to describe myself. But now I had an out.

"There isn't time," I said. "Hold on tight now, here we go down . . ."

Chapter Eight

Varan was right in his forecast—the Xarthian War did not last long.

It might have been over even quicker if Mannheim had not suddenly had an attack of self-righteousness and swung the Ship's Council to back him. Our skipper said he wanted to "make Middle Sector safe for democracy," and therefore he demanded that the Xarthians surrender unconditionally. The Emperor, I think, was on the point of being assassinated by his own nobles when they learned our terms—and then they rallied round him, and resistance stiffened.

Our terms, incidentally, were conveyed with the greatest of ease. Kanyo told us that Elders at the court of Xarth would convey the necessary text. When Belmondo wanted to know how those Elders would get our message, Kanyo said coolly:

"We Elders have mental methods of communication. They are instantaneous . . ."

When I translated this, the First Officer's eyes bugged.

"Telepathic radio! Is he serious?"

"I think so," I said, remembering how Telesin had

known all about my doings 300 miles up the canal within hours of the events. "The Abbot Dlan tried to hedge with tales about heliographs and so on, but the Queen herself told me it's the Elders who are the main news service on Xuma—and they certainly don't use radio or we'd have detected their broadcasts. The Xuman armies do use light signals, because the Elders will help only when they think the cause is a very good one; but mirror-flashing is a slow process and anyway the system is a bit disorganized just now, because of the chaos on the canals leading to Xarth. I guess we can rely on the Elders' system—it worked perfectly in my case."

"This needs looking into," said Belmondo. "O.K., we'll try the medicine men, but I'd like to see them while they're *transmitting*."

When I translated this to Kanyo, he demurred.

"Our sender needs complete privacy," he said. "The least distraction, you realize . . ."

Well, we played it their way, and we immediately got an answer via Kanyo. He reported that the subject cities of Nakaan and Hiraxa were in full revolt, but the Xarthians were defying us. Kanyo read from the tula-paper on which one of his scribes had jotted down the return message:

"The Emperor and his loyal subjects are not afraid of sky demons. The powers of the true gods will destroy them, and Heaven will smile upon Xarth again. Death rather than surrender!"

"Now we've got a chance to check whether this mumbo jumbo *works*," said Belmondo—and sent off a couple of landers to reconnoiter Nakaan and Hiraxa. In a few hours they were back. Yes—the two cities were waving their own flags on their roof tops; they were also hoisting skull-masked heads on the points of spears, and driving skull-masked troops away from their gates. But Xarth looked orderly, and on the roof tops of the city skull-masked warriors were waving their swords, brandishing their red dragon banner, and yelling defiance as the strange craft swooped over.

"Okay, so it *does* work," said Belmondo. "When we've got this planet sorted out, we'll have to have a full investigation of the method. Maybe Weiser can figure it out. It should be of great military value back in the Sol system. Now, as for this Zarth dump . . ."

It was horrible, but we could not stop it: Belmondo and Mannheim acted too quickly for us to protest, under the *emergency* provisions of the ship's rules—even though there was no emergency. I guess Mannheim had been itching to test his big laser on a genuine target. So, suddenly, about a quarter of the city of Xarth ceased to exist.

That casual furnace breath from the sky cut a swathe of emptiness half a kilometer wide through the city wall, through houses, markets, gardens and monasteries of Elders, until it emerged from the other side of the city and the gunner three thousand miles up took his finger off the trigger; and then the fires began. Xarth is a main junction of the planet-wide canal system, and the city's canal pump house was wiped out, and the whole system in Middle Sector partly disrupted. There would probably be a famine in the territory of our Tlanash allies that winter because of what had happened at Xarth.

Ironically, the palace of the Emperor Retumon remained unscathed.

"We can get him next time round if necessary," grinned Belmondo. "Hell, that was only a delicate hint . . ."

Jack Willis spoke up sharply. The tall fair-haired engineer was on quite good terms with Belmondo and his crowd—at least he was till that moment. But he did get it through the thick heads of our space marines that you simply couldn't go about lasering a Xuman city here and there without terrible repercussions on the general planetary ecology.

"Hell, it's like busting a main ponic tube up in *Horse*," he protested; "the shit flies all over the place. That may frighten the enemy, but for chrissake, it's gonna panic our friends as well, and maybe we still do want a few friends on this planet."

So it was now agreed that we didn't have to laser Xarth again; in its present condition we should be able to take the place with a modest surprise air attack. And that was what we did.

We flew to Xarth with all five of our lander ships, the bellies of the craft packed full of Yelsai's best guardsmen. I acted as flight leader, and I had Varan and two young warriors packed in with me. Actually, once we were airborne, I let Varan fly. He handled the ship so well that when we got to the enemy city I let him continue as pilot, while I concentrated on the laser cannon. I guess Belmondo and the other pilots thought I was both flying and shooting, which is just possible with the smallest landers.

We circled the Emperor's palace. There were quite a few skull-masked warriors on the flat roof. You had to admire their bravery, as all around them the city was half ruined, with fires blazing in half a dozen places. But as we came in close, we could see little red figures running away from the palace at ground level. Belmondo flew his ship low over these, and wiped them out.

Then Varan flew me over the palace roof, and I waggled the laser, and that was that. The roof was clear of living enemies.

"So very simple," said Varan grimly, looking at me as we flew back again. "Now you fly, Tomass: this is the hard part—we must get down there."

Belmondo stayed on his death-patrol to see that no one got away from the palace, but the rest of us landed on the roof, using the vertical jets. Out poured the Yelsai troops; and I went with them. The other pilots thought I was nuts, I guess—they stayed where they were, to look after their ships and preserve their valuable colonist lives. But I went into that building, with Varan just ahead of me, rushing down the stairs.

The Xarthian imperial palace was not very like the royal palace of Yelsai. The rooms were higher, more grandiose, and the corridors long and ornamented with a motif of huge red dragons on white and sometimes even black walls. But we had not come there to admire the decor.

We found ourselves almost at once in a long gloomy corridor from which there opened a succession of small curtained doorways. At a few of these doors, I saw the faces of Xuman girls peeping out; the corridor itself was barred by Xarthian warriors, who were being driven back by Varan's men.

"Stand aside!" I shouted, and when the Yelsai guards threw themselves against the walls, I fanned my laser. The Xarthians crumpled, and the girls screamed and vanished. But Varan dived in at the nearest doorway and came back almost at once dragging a girl by the wrist. She was heavily made up, and wore a lot of jewels and bracelets and not much else.

"Where?" said Varan.

"Just beyond this corridor," said the girl, pointing.

Varan let go of her wrist, and turned to me. "Tomass, I would be obliged if you would lower your death-thrower now. Keep it for your own protection. We are sufficient swordsmen, and the Emperor's throne room lies at the end of this passage."

"O.K., let's go," I said.

At the entrance to the throne room we found a fresh batch of Xarthians, but Varan's boys soon drove them in—and then, there was the Emperor himself, protected by only a handful of women generals. Our Yelsaians took on the women, but Varan reserved the Emperor for his own sword.

Retumon was a powerfully-built kurar: in Earth terms, he looked a well-preserved forty, and he was no slouch with a sword either. He made one furious rush at young Varan—I raised my laser, but it was too late, they were so bunched up together and moving so quickly that I could not possibly fire without endangering the Prince.

I never did see what happened. A second later Retumon gasped and staggered back, with blood on his mouth: I think Varan caught him a blow with his hilt. But he was not seriously hurt, and then the bout really began.

After a minute or two, the women generals were all dead or had surrendered, but Varan made his own men stand back, and leave him and the Emperor to fight it out. Finally, he cornered Retumon up against the back of his throne, and ran him through with one clean thrust—just like in the history-fiction movies we used to see in Lunaris or in *Riverhorse.*

That boy was a real hero, you see. It's funny how the type doesn't alter much, not even across twenty light-years.

And now, of course, the war was over. Within the hour, we had a nervous deputation of Xarthian nobles and merchants coming to us in the Palace and signifying their surrender. Belmondo wanted to proclaim that the city was not part of the Empire of Yelsai, but Varan refused.

"My mother has instructed me—she doesn't want to be Empress of Xarth," he said.

Then one of the Xarthians spoke up. He was a kurar, and a noble of high rank, as I judged from his blood-red kilt and lavish gold ornaments.

"It has been our custom," he said grimly, "that the slayer of our Emperor becomes the next Emperor. Our state has long been a cosmopolitan one, and foreign birth has been no bar to high office. For example, Retumon was originally a foreign slave, born and bought in Kvaryla. Now, this gallant young prince is no slave, and he has the right qualification; if he will accept the title . . ."

And the next moment the merchants were all chorusing:

"Varan, Emperor! Varan, Emperor of Xarth!"

Varan smiled. "I cannot be an Emperor, since there is no longer an Empire. Hiraxa and Nakaan are now independent cities, and it is good that they should be so. But if you wish, I will accept some more modest title . . ."

In the end they revived an old title from earlier Xarth history, and proclaimed him *Alkityo-danyel,* which meant something like "Prince Protector."

"I hope I can truly protect you," said Varan soberly. "You realize, the star folk will be the real rulers of this city now? As indeed of all Xuman cities."

"What did they say?" asked Belmondo.

"He said," I interpreted, "that we gods from the stars were the real protectors of this city, since it was we who liberated them from the tyranny of that frightful Emperor."

Belmondo grinned, and patted Varan on the head.

"Good boy," he said. "It's nice when the natives are sensible, and grateful."

And now that the Great Xarthian War was over, a certain sense of relaxation came to the new 'gods' of Xuma.

The landers were kept busy now, and more and more *dinoy* descended from the star Vepan to the Fort before Yel Karagor, the Gate of Dragons. Oh yes, *dinoy*—I don't know who coined the word, it wasn't yet in any Xuman dictionary kept by the Elders, but it was spreading among the populace of Yelsai. Not *aan*, "gods," but *dinoy*, "moonfaces"—or should I say "palefaces"?

Well, gods or palefaces, the point occurred to many of us almost simultaneously that there was no longer any urgency about Plan 2/3/A—perhaps, really, there never had been. When your armament so enormously outclasses anything in the rest of the world, why bother with subtle strategies? Why "divide and rule" when you can rule anyway?

Certainly, after the battle of Xarth, it was obvious that the whole of Xuma was ours for the asking. All we had to do was come down and inspect our winnings. And this we could do at our leisure.

But—we were really very, very few. Pitifully few. It was great to have a whole planet at our command—and yet it was reassuring to huddle together, as if for protection. That was why Mannheim got the policy adopted, that at all times the bulk of our people should be either up in *Riverhorse*—which was safety itself—or in Yelsai, where the natives were friendly and grateful for our intervention. And normally the Earthfolk in Yelsai would be in the Fort—especially the women, the future breeders of our race on this planet.

At least, that was the theory at first. After a few weeks, as we began to get used to Xuma, and to feel more at ease in Yelsai, more and more people began to break these rules and to call for modifications of them.

For one thing, it was obvious that we had to have some sort of permanent presence in the Yelsai palace. I, especially, as Xuman-language expert had to be there a lot, *and,* I'm happy to say, Sally made out an impressive case for sticking around the palace too—she said she wanted to check up on Saimo's physical development. And Dave Weiser wanted to check Saimo's new psychology, and investigate the telepathic powers of those palace elders; and Rosa promptly declared she had to study the ecology of the Palace roof garden, a quite unique environment. . . .

And Belmondo didn't want to leave all us liberals and native-lovers on our own, so . . . so finally we had another Fort on the roof of the Palace. Gradually, I'm afraid, Queen Telesin and her people were moved out of the penthouse block altogether, and the Queen's bedchamber was reserved for Mannheim or Belmondo on their visits; and part of the roof garden was demolished (in spite of Rosa's protests) to make a landing space for the smaller and lighter of our flying craft.

I asked Varan once what he thought of all this. He smiled bitterly, and said:

"It is inevitable, Tomass. My teacher Kanyo used to tell me never to grieve over the inevitable. He would say, 'Consider the *golas,* the trade balloons. How does a trader from Yelsai reach the rich lands of the East? The trade wind blows *from* the east. Does he try to fly against the wind? No—he goes with it; and the world is round; and therefore by going always west, he comes at last to the most desirable eastern kingdoms. That is the emblem of all time, all change.' So Kanyo used to say; and so it must be now with us."

"That sounds mysterious to me," I said. "*We* are going to have a look at the Eastern cities, by and by, we moonfaces, and we are going to fly directly eastward to do it. The ability of brute power, you see."

I paused. There was something bothering me in what Varan had just said, and now I realized. He had used a certain verb particle (*vy:* remote past) in speaking of Kanyo; and I had not seen Kanyo since—when was it? Yes, the day Mannheim had lasered Xarth. I asked Varan what had happened to the old Counsellor.

"The Order recalled him to Khadan," he said. "I presume they want a first-hand account of you star-folk. I hope they will let Kanyo return, or else Psyl will be grieved—and so will I."

"Why, he should have asked us for transport," I exclaimed, "we could get him there much faster, and I know Belmondo and Mannheim want to investigate Khadan soon anyway . . ."

Varan shrugged. "Perhaps time is not all that important. What is a few weeks or months in the history of our planet?"

What indeed? As I say, we were getting the same idea ourselves, we moonfaces. We had been cooped up in that starship for three years of lived time, plus eight years of nonexistence on ice, and now . . . now we could relax. Not many of us wanted to fly missions round the world when we had the strange new living city of Yelsai and its grateful natives right on our doorsteps. We put up a case for in-depth research, before we went on the big expeditions, into the local technology, science, mores . . .

Jack Willis and his girl Sheila McIntyre moved onto the Palace roof. Jack was officially supposed to be investigating canal hydraulics; and Sheila was officially assisting Rosa with her work on the tula plant. With Dave and Sally and I that made six of us special friends, with six separate roof rooms (officially). In those first days, we did not work very hard, let me tell you. As some ancient poet once said, Bliss was it in that dawn to be alive. I don't suppose *he* had lived all his life in artificial atmospheres, with black death the thickness of a deck or a dome away; or spent eight years a frozen semi-corpse; but anyway, he was prophet enough to express what we all felt.

Research? No, we did not do all that much research at that time—except research into the sensation of being alive, truly alive, like healthy animals.

Well, there was *one* popular area of research among some moonfaces, though none of my immediate friends—practical research into the matter of Xuman sexuality. And many of our boys began to investigate this especially in the House of the Spring Fire-fish. I may say that since Varan achieved power and status, he had got his mother and the Ladies to pass a law freeing all kynthi and kurar from their former condition of state slavery; but not many of the Fire-fish inmates had taken up the option of leaving their accustomed trade. So there was still plenty of scope there for the kind of research I have mentioned. I know what the Xuman girls found out—i.e. that "gods" were lousy lovers; but they had been trained to flatter their customers, so our boys came away from there with their egos boosted, and pretty well satisfied. After all, the little red kids were nearly as good as human women for that business, and so very much more sweetly submissive . . . A few of them tried it also with *kun* women, for instance the mature and obliging dancers; but somehow this did not work so well, in fact the red ladies were inclined to jeer, so after that our fellows stuck to the delectable little kynthi.

And in spite of Belmondo's chest-beating, I know that some of our *girls* experimented, too—especially the ones who were supposed to be penned up in the airport Fort. Sally was biologist enough to know that it was hopeless, and told them so, but quite a few wouldn't take her word for it. I'm afraid there were soon some very frustrated young guardsmen around the Yelsai Palace, and two or three Earth girls had to go to Sally for medical attention . . . Quickly the news spread through Middle Sector that 'goddesses' were perhaps beautiful, and very willing, but quite impenetrable. In spite of being purely and forever feminine, they had to be worshipped only from afar . . .

For many of us, though, at all times the best of sex and love was to be had from *each other*. One decision we Earth folk took quietly, unanimously, and at once. While in space we had had the sex, of course, but there had been a taboo on breeding. Now that ban was lifted. In the week after the end of the war, a half dozen of our four dozen female crew members started babies, and many more were trying. And every day almost, some couple or other were getting married.

Sally had a very pleasant room in the palace, and she had made it almost home-like—i.e. like her pad in

Riverhorse, with stuff she had brought down from the ship, including a tape recorder and a micro-reader and a supply of my favorite microbooks. One afternoon—we had just made love, and Sally was getting us a cup of *tlaok*-coffee from the Xuman child who served us—she was taking the tray at the door and I was lying on the bed reading a micro, and chuckling.

"What's so funny?" she said, closing the door and putting down the tray.

"The way they get married on Barsoom. It really is wedlock there! Metal collars and chains, padlocked together!"

"That might have its points," grinned Sally, "but the Xuman ceremony is nice too. I did think it was touching—yeah, literally—when Saimo and Varan held up their hands the other day, palm to palm. Why can't we humans do that too?"

"'My woman for all six days of the week,'" I quoted. "But we haven't got six fingers, so the symbolism would be spoilt. I'd just as soon sign a dicto-form with you, Sal, next time Mannheim is handy."

Sally was still and silent for a moment. Then she said evenly: "Does that mean you are proposing permanency, Tom Carson? Seriously? For us?"

"Sure," I said, "why not? Dave and Rosa, and Jack and Sheila, are all going to—I don't see why we should be left out. I think we're suited, don't you?"

"Oh, I do, I do," she said, throwing her arms round me and kissing me with enthusiasm.

"Hey," I said, "what about that cup of coffee?"

I'm sorry if that doesn't sound romantic. Quite right, it *doesn't* sound romantic. But there you are—that's how it happened. I didn't kneel to Sally, or call her "my princess," or rescue her from the clutches of some depraved alien tyrant by my tremendous ability as a swordsman, smashing empires and killing millions of people in the process. But then, I never did claim to be a hero—and Sally wasn't that kind of heroine. She was just a damn nice girl and one I liked a hell of a lot, and she liked me too, and—well, as I told her, we did suit each other, and I'm damn glad I married her—which I

David J. Lake

did a week later in a most unromantic ceremony administered by skipper Mannheim and his secretary.

And now I might say a few words about the Xuman women I had known—how they were getting on about this time. Psyl shouldn't be counted here, I suppose, but I always thought of her as a woman. Well, she was polite to us *dinoy*, but she seemed tense, and I knew she was missing Kanyo, Telesin . . .

Ah, poor Telesin. Since that one hectic, disappointing night, she had always seemed a little sad, quiet—almost, you might say, older. She was taking Xuman lovers again, now a normal boy from the guards, now a kurar captain, but by all accounts not as often as she used to. She seemed to be doing it more as if to prove something than for the pleasure itself.

Saimo, on the other hand, was blossoming. Princess Saimo of Xarth she was now, and she kept receiving visitors from her old thon 2-3-6 who came to admire her—including, oddly, her former stepfather, now turned a pretty young *woman* who got herself taken on as a lady-in-waiting to the Princess, her former stepchild. Xuman biology—it still throws me at times! But Saimo herself, now: she now definitely looked beautiful and feminine. She had well-formed breasts and dainty nipples, which of course were always visible, whether she wore a simple skirt or a high-collared "Cretan" gown. It was a pleasure to see her with Varan—hell, it was a pleasure to see her anyway. And what was nice was that she was still fond of me in a certain fashion.

But I'm glad we never tried anything together. Physical sex with an alien species is definitely a mistake. One doesn't have to have that: one can have love instead, which is better.

PART THREE

The Divine Fire

Chapter Nine

One of the subtler pleasures of those early days on Ares-Xuma was flying in astroplanes, aero mode. Eventually we set out to explore the planet by personal inspection of certain key spots. We groaned a bit at having to leave Yelsai, home and beauty on these missions, but there were definite compensations—such as, seeing the blue-green line of the canal snaking away to the horizon in a delicate curve, with wisps of mist marking its course; and the red desert below, with its ridges and wrinkles, so like the red deserts of Mars or Australia; and overhead, over everything, the dark sapphire of that lonely Eridanian sky. At our cruising height and jet speed, Xuma was clearly a sphere, a small round planet, smaller than Earth, and yet amply wider than Luna or even Old Mars.

On the first day of Second Month (local style), I found myself flying to Khadan. Since there are only 24 days in a Xuman month, this was just three Earth weeks after my first landing on the planet, and barely two Xuman weeks (12 days) after the end of the Xarthian war.

We flew in a couple of astro-landers—Dave, Jack

133

Willis and I in a medium-sized one, and Mannheim, Belmondo and four marines, all armed to the teeth, in the other larger model. This was only Mannheim's second spell down on the surface, and he was more uneasy about Xumans than most of us: he had insisted on coming in force in the big lander to "give us covering fire" if necessary.

It certainly wouldn't be necessary. Khadan, Psyl had told us, was one of the most unmilitary spots on all Xuma, a complex of monasteries and canal works, all inhabited by grey-skinned venerable elders. For over two million years the place had been dedicated to peace and the preservation of life; there wasn't even a sword or a bow and arrow anywhere in this alien Vatican or Lhasa.

As we drew nearer, "Lhasa" seemed the better comparison. The desert below changed from red to grey to the white of snow. The sky above, as we came down lower, was veiled with wintry clouds; and when we struck the line of Meridian Canal, and flew down really low, we saw a crust of ice on that thin straight waterway. In this season of the southern winter, the canal was not flowing: it was the northern ice cap that was melting now, and supplying the life-giving waters to the cities nearer the Equator. We were coming to Khadan in the off season.

"That's it, I guess," said Jack, pointing out the front window at some specks of black against the general whiteness. "Well, the sooner we get there, the sooner we get it over with." Like Dave and me, Jack had been married to his girl precisely yesterday. So none of us wanted to spend the night in Khadan . . .

Our basic mission, of course, was technological espionage—if you can call "espionage" what you do quite openly. We had already been at this for the past two weeks in Yelsai—without a great deal of success. Oh, sure, the local elders had shown us everything—at least, it looked that way—their monasteries, their schools, shops, factories, and the pumping houses for the canals. On the whole, we had been able to classify their technology as about equal to that of the Earth in the late

18th Century, but with some big discrepancies either way. For instance—

Plenty of metals, as one might expect on a small planet, and notably a lot of gold, which formed the basis of the coinage and credit. An advanced theoretical chemistry, but no knowledge of gunpowder or other explosives. Theoretical knowledge of steam engines, but no large-scale practical applications, perhaps for lack of suitable fuel—possibly the planet had never had a carboniferous age—anyway, fossil fuels appeared to be lacking. Electricity they did have—they called it "atom-sex," treating electrons as *male* and protons as *female,* and even speculating about "pervert matter"—i.e. antimatter, positrons being "kynthi-particles"; but again, they didn't make much use of electricity, not having enough brute power to make dynamos worthwhile. Their best power seemed to be water power, when the canals were flowing fastest in the spring. Oh yes, and they did have wind pumps.

What was amusing was that *all* the advanced technology in Yelsai was in the hands of the elders. Certain products—such as helium for trading balloons—well, the elders sold them to lay folk and so financed their local monasteries. Why the lay folk never thought to get into the production themselves remained a bit of a mystery. Maybe it was just tradition—turning out helium etcetera was a thing one just didn't do when young. Everyone would be an elder one day, and then you could go into science and so on if that was where your skill lay.

"I don't expect we'll find anything startling here, beyond bigger and better canal works," said Jack. "More in your line, I guess, Dave."

Dave Weiser scratched his head. "Maybe . . . I wish I could make some progress on this alleged telepathy. Every time I asked Psyl or any of the other oldies about it, I got the feeling they were wrapping it up in a lot of half-baked mysticism. They sound like a bunch of post-Jungians . . . The Abbot of that big monastery near the Dragon Gate just smiled wisely and said '*tulan*.' That simply means 'communication,' doesn't it, Tom?"

"I guess so," I said. "The root is *tul-*, same as in the tula plant. I presume the connection is that tula leaves are used for paper, and paper for written messages."

"Talk of the devil," grinned Jack, pointing.

We were coming in now for our landing, on a wide patch of bare ground before the black main pile of monastery buildings. All around this area was a huge complex of waterways, mostly crusted with ice: dams, barrages, pump houses, and the beginnings of three canals running north, east and west. From this one vital spot, in the southern spring, there would go forth the melt-waters to the three great Sectors of Xuma, Middle, East and West, keeping the planet alive and at least partly green while the north-polar waters were sealed by frost. And, we now saw, there were lines of tula plants marching up from those canals, past the pump houses, circling our landing area, and disappearing into or behind the monastery block.

"It certainly is a hell of a plant," said Dave, frowning at the tula as though it concealed some mystery which baffled him. "Very hardy, my Rosa says. I suppose it is frost resistant."

"O.K.," I said, "here we are." And I landed the ship close to the monastery block, while Belmondo came down a hundred meters farther off.

We were expected—Psyl had told us we would be. Out from the buildings came a small group of white-robed elders.

Once we were out of the lander, the cold hit us like a giant icy fist. We had expected that, and were well wrapped up in furs. It was the smiling, bowing elders who shocked me: they were bare-legged, bare-armed, and seemed to be wearing only their standard thin white robes. As soon as we had made the introductions, I commented on this.

The thin-faced green-eyed one who called himself Aoak smiled briefly. "We have our little secrets, To-mass Carson: tricks of our trade, you might say. It is true that our species is more cold-resistant than yours, but these robes of ours are not quite of the Yelsai type. They are lined with the pitch of tula. It is an excellent insulator."

Insulator, I thought. Aoak had used the word *la-xi*, which basically meant "no move," i.e. "stopper"—one of the Yelsai elders had used the same word in describing the sheathing of one of his primitive electric leads. I began to get an idea.

"Hey, Tom, how about a bit of translation?" said Jack.

I was thinking furiously. The same problem I had been facing for weeks was cropping up again—which side was I on? And which side were Jack and Dave on? They were my friends, yes; and they disliked the way Mannheim's gang were treating the Xumans, yes; but we had not seriously discussed politics, I hadn't told them about my rather special relationship with Prince Varan, and, frankly, I didn't know if they would agree to a definite coverup.

I cleared my throat. "Aoak says their clothes are lined with tula pith. It is very cold-resistant."

The moment passed: Jack made no comment; and now Mannheim's party was joining us. Almost at once I was convinced that telepathy was a sham. I had been trying so hard *not* to think of a certain simple idea, that if telepathy really existed I felt sure Jack would have picked up my thought about *tula insulators*. Of course, the Xuman elders might be much greater adepts than we; but the whole history of human experiments in ESP had shown that the power was a damned chancy thing. And the reliability, the detail of the messages the Xuman elders had been sending . . . No. I was damn sure my hunch was right. But I was going to keep it to myself.

Well, we got shown round Khadan that day—it was a bit of a lightning tour. Most of the time Jack was off away from the rest of us inspecting the canal works with a couple of grey-skinned technicians; the marines stayed in the landers nursing our major firepower; and Dave and I and the brass inspected the main monastery. The brass were not impressed.

"If you've seen one Artian monkery, you've seen them all," said Belmondo; and Mannheim nodded agreement.

Dave and I felt differently. Khadan was big and cold,

bare and massive, but in its austere way, very beautiful. There were great halls where monks sat in silence, wrapped in profound meditation; and little chapels, used for private prayer or rituals; and council chambers, and scriptoria, and elegant refectories with frescoed walls (the frescoes being all abstracts—lines, circles and sunbursts in black, white and gold). One whole wing was devoted to the reception of novice pilgrims—newly-turned Elders who made the long trip from the equatorial cities up the canals to this polar retreat—a bit like those fictional Barsoomians seeking their Lost Sea of Korus (but Xuma has no lost seas, nor lost anything: after 2+ million years of civilization and balloon travel, the planet is extremely well mapped, and there is no room on its surface to mislay so much as a fish pond).

Aoak seemed to be the leader of the group of elders who were hosting us: in fact, he admitted to being a member of the inner council, the so-called Supreme Court of Poetry. He was also the Official Chronicler.

"Ah," I said, "that Chronicle! I've heard of it. Can you show it to us?"

"Follow me," said Aoak. And soon we were standing in the great Scriptorium of the Chronicle. This vast hall contained the only two copies of the Chronicle of Years that were kept at Khadan—one the hand-written, calligraphic copy, the other a single copy of the printed edition. There were so many volumes of each that they filled nearly all the shelf space in the huge room.

"Why," said Dave, "you're soon gonna have to knock down the wall for next year's installment."

When I translated this, Aoak said, "Perhaps. That is if our history does continue."

Dave was already making a bee-line for Volume One.

"What does this say?" he asked, opening at the first page of the hand-written version.

Aoak took the book gently from his hand, and read in that beautiful strange tenor voice that is common to all Elders:

" 'The Beginning of the Tale of Years, and Summary of the Year Zero, by Nyken, Scribe and Elder. Truly, says Wisdom, there can never be a first beginning, since every line is part of that great circle which makes up eternity. But within the circle there are some points which it is convenient and fitting to treat as beginnings. Therefore have we, of the One United Order of Elders, decided to count a new era from this year, in which we have established ourselves as a single band of siblings, owing loyalty not to a queen here, or to a city there, but to Xuma herself, our poor tormented mother, trusting that by our efforts and our love we may save the life of our world. May there be many more years to count; and even though our hope for that is not great, it is better than no hope at all. At least the worst crisis may now be past, now that the gods and the demons are departed: so long as they do not return, so long as their chariots are not seen again in heaven, the ravaged earth *(xu)* may blossom, the mother *(ma)* may bring forth children, the blighted life of Xuma may revive if only for a time . . ."

"Aoak, stop!" I cried. "When was this piece actually written?"

"Why, at the end of the Year Zero. That is the custom we have retained ever since—to review the year at the end of the year. Of course, this volume I hold in my hand was not physically written then—it has been copied and recopied, and the language modernized. But substantially, these are the words of our first Chronicler, the elder Nyken."

"Then, if this is not a legend—can you tell me please, what *did* happen in your Year Zero—or rather, before it? Who were these gods and demons who had departed, and what had they done to Xuma?"

Aoak said, evenly: "I will tell you, O Children of the Hamlor. The ancient gods and demons—they were two races of star folk. One was in appearance not unlike Xumans, or like you people. Our ancestors called them 'gods,' and when you first landed on Xuma we thought it was they, the gods, who had returned. Now we do not think that. The other race . . ." He paused, and his expression darkened. "They were nothing like you or like us, and the stories told of them are very terrible. They were, above all, enemies of the gods. Their chariots landed on Xuma a few hours before the gods came, and in those few hours the demons destroyed a dozen cities and laid waste whole lands. I should explain that in those days Xuma was not like it is now—there was deep water filling the oceans, and there were broad green lands where there is now nothing but red desert.

"Perhaps even the demons would not have hurt Xuma beyond healing if they had been unopposed, for in fact they were not much interested in our world. They were using it only as a stopping place on a long journey, they came from the Dragon's breathings—"

"The Magellan Clouds?" I gasped. "Go on."

"And they were going to attack the gods somewhere in the heart of things, the center of our galaxy. But the gods were not taken by surprise: they came out from the Great Center, and they smote the demons. Unfortunately for us, they smote them on Xuma and around Xuma. During that terrible battle one of our moons—for we then had two—one of our moons was battered out of its former orbit, and broke up to form the belt of Whirling Stars. Also, our oceans were vaporized, and most of our people died.

"The only consolation we had was that the gods won that battle. Their great ships—some of them—remained near Xuma for a little while afterwards, and it was they who helped to save us from total destruction; otherwise I think not one Xuman would have survived. Then—then the gods went away; and they have never returned."

My colleagues were by this time fairly dancing with impatience, so I had to stop Aoak and translate the whole fantastic story.

"Crap," said Belmondo.

"Mumbo jumbo," said Mannheim. "If these space-travelling 'gods' have been around for the last two-and-a-half million years, where the hell are they now?"

I put this question to Aoak. He spread his hands.

"We do not know. Most likely, they have remained among their home worlds."

"What home worlds?"

"The Great Center—the Heart of Being—the middle of our galaxy. While they were rescuing our ancestors, the gods told them that normally their ships did not come so far out into these poor, thin regions of space where stars are so far apart. Their intention at that time was to exterminate the demon race, and then retire to their own beautiful and closely clustering worlds. And that, we think, is what they have done."

I translated, and then turned back to the elder. "Tell me more," I said. "What were these gods like, to look at?"

"Very like you," said Aoak, "but maybe taller. The stories say, nine feet high, and the pictures show them as gold-skinned, orange-haired, with eyes like fire. They lived by nature for two thousand years, and then they would cast themselves into magic baths and emerge as young as ever. One tale says that even their children had sex, so perhaps they were more like you than like us." He paused. "Is it really true, Tomass Carson, that you of the Hamlor-world do not live longer than us? Only a hundred years, or less?"

"It is true," I said.

"That amazes me," said Aoak. "The gods told our ancestors that *all* races which travelled among the stars lived for at least one thousand years, and some for much more. Those frightful demons, for example, had no natural death at all. It had to be so, according to the gods—because the distances between the stars were so great that short-livers could not span them by any tolerable methods. And yet, you are here!"

"Maybe our methods are *not* tolerable, at that," I murmured.

"It is also strange," he continued, "another way. According to our thinking, it is always the Center which must dominate the periphery. So the gods, being of the Center, dominated the demons, and crushed them. Yet now *you* dominate Xuma from your little whirling star on the fringes of our world! There is something in this situation that is most unnatural . . ."

I translated once more, and again Mannheim and Belmondo were totally unimpressed. But as for me, in spite of the cold, I had begun to sweat.

Aoak's story hung together with everything I already knew of Xuma. By all indications, the oceans *had* vanished only two-and-a-half million years ago, and only that much time was needed to account for the Ring-Belt. Certainly there had been some vast catastrophe—and Aoak's explanation of it was plausible. Come to think of it, it also explained one or two features of ancient Earthly mythology. The gods and the demons .. *And there was war in heaven* ...

We humans with our little "Operation Breakout"! What if we attracted the attention of those galactic *true* gods of Xuma? Then there might be a vast Operation Break-*in* ...

We had lunch in the great refectory. Mannheim of course fed samples of everything to a Taster before passing it as fit for our consumption; but everything was. During the meal Dave inquired once more into the elders' powers of ESP.

"You must meet Ayun, our sensitive, our prophet," said Aoak.

And after lunch, we did. Ayun was a frail little elder who inhabited a small bare cell. He seemed afraid when he saw us. Apparently he had predicted our coming several months before we entered planetary orbit. But Ayun could not explain how he did it—he uttered prophecies only when in trance (I think, under self-hypnosis), and claimed to be unconscious of what he was saying at the time.

The Khadan elders did have a theory to explain away the paradox of prophecy. Aoak said, "A prophet does not predict: he merely draws on the memory of the universe. For time is circular, therefore what will be has been, therefore ..."

But this sort of thing was not in my line. It left Dave gasping, too.

There were a couple of things we *didn't* see in Khadan. No High Lama or Pope, no single Chief Elder. The top guys were that Council of Twelve, who called themselves the Supreme Court of Poetry. Well, judging poetry was *one* of their functions; I had strong suspicions that they had other powers, too, but I didn't press the point.

The other lacuna was simply—Kanyo. I asked Aoak about him, but Aoak seemed not to know. "Probably he has not yet arrived," he said. "From Yelsai to Khadan—that is a great many miles for a pilgrim on foot, and the ways are bitter at this season."

When we had finished, and were walking out over that cold bare ground to our flying craft, Mannheim said, "Why do they have only this *one* feeder from the south polar cap, when the north has three?"

Jack explained, "Most of the South Pole area is a depression—a former ocean. It doesn't drain northwards. But just south of here is a plateau above the ex-ocean, and this is the one place where melt-water can easily be collected. That's why Khadan is more of a crucial spot than the three northern snow monasteries."

"Worth remembering," said Mannheim. "If we threatened to laser this place, we could hold the whole planet up to ransom."

"Aren't we doing that already?" I said.

Chapter Ten

As soon as we got back to Yelsai, Mannheim left us to go "topside," i.e. back to *Riverhorse*. The starship was an unpopular place to be, these days, and it was manned only by a skeleton crew—mostly laser-gunners. The women in particular, once they had seen the surface of Xuma, could not be persuaded to go back. But Mannheim felt differently—he was quite happy in the echoing emptiness that was now his own command. He also had kept back a handful of women, not letting them land yet. This may have been partly to give comfort to his orbiting troops; partly, he said, he didn't like "putting all our eggs in one basket." (I really loved his metaphor!) For the women were the future mothers of our race on Xuma. In the nature of things, because nothing can exceed the speed of light, any appeal by us for reinforcements from the Solar System must remain fruitless for over forty-five years.

"It's not likely," said Mannheim in one of his broadcasts from the ship, "that we'll see any new human faces on Ares in our own lifetimes—except the faces of our children. That's why we've got to *breed*. Breed fast, and careful. Populate or perish. And that's why, men, we've got to take great, great care of our womenfolk. This ship is by far the safest place, and I intend always to keep *some* women here. Next best are the two Yelsai establishments, Airport and Palace, and I'm relying on you guys down there to see that all the girls are never in just *one* of them at any one time. By the same token, women are *not*, repeat *not*, to go on any exploring missions to other cities."

"Oh *yeah*?" growled Sally, "who says?"

The fact was, I was scheduled to go off pretty well at once on a round-the-planet snooping trip; and so were Dave and Jack and several other guys. *Their* wives or girlfriends kicked too; but this time the majority of our colonists sided with Mannheim. The snooping parties had to go stag.

Immediately, we were going to make a tour of the East Sector, then the West, and so come back to Yelsai. The idea this time was not to uncover dangerous technology—we were pretty well convinced by now (most of us) that the Xumans had none—but to look for desirable residences for us lords of the world. Yelsai was getting a bit chilly now as the southern winter wore on, and the lush East and semi-lush West Sectors beckoned. Both were on or north of the Equator, sandwiched between a couple of landlocked "ocean" depressions—the East Sector between the North Ocean (Laral Lýl) and the East Ocean (Laral Ao), the West Sector between the East and West Oceans.

I had to go, of course, because I was still the only "god" with any good command of the native language. The other key interpreter, Saimo, was now with her husband Prince Varan in Xarth, and we were going to pick her up on the first leg of our flight—whether Varan liked it or not.

"Hell, he can always come too," said Belmondo. "Maybe he would be good propaganda, too, in the East—he can tell them what we did to Xarth."

The night before we took off I had a private interview with Psyl. She looked at me bright-eyed when I told her I hadn't seen Kanyo at Khadan.

"I do not really fear for his safety," she said. "Kanyo seems gentle, but deep down he is very tough. Even

145

when we were both young and I was that one's husband, my wife was no timid little kynthi like these warped creatures of Yelsai. You will perhaps see others like that if you visit our city, Xulpona, Tomass."

I laughed. "That always throws me—the way you people take turns at being both sexes. Well, Psyl, I suppose you will have everything fixed up for our reception along the route—via your usual *grapevine*."

I had used the English word. Psyl looked startled.

"Grapevine? Tomass, I have been studying your language—is not that a plant?"

"A long, trailing plant," I agreed. "It also signifies a means of communication—rather like your tula."

She sat very still and silent.

"Don't worry," I told her. "Anything I suspect about your folk, or your secret organization, Psyl—I won't tell a soul. I'm on your side, Psyl."

She stared at me. "Yes—I think you are, partly," she said slowly. "But how far?"

"When it comes to resistance—well, my grandfather was a member of a resistance movement. I'm with you all the way, Psyl."

"Impossible," she said. "No member of an invading people can be with the natives 'all the way.' Not unless he has a very unusual gift for treachery."

I shook my head. "Hasn't Varan told you anything about me?"

"Yes. He has told me that you are a very decent person. And therefore my previous statement still stands."

"I really don't understand you," I said.

"I'm glad of that," said Psyl. She stretched out her grey wrinkled hand, and touched mine. "Dear Tomass, there may be a day when we can be quite frank with each other. But that day is not yet. Now, please go. If you see Kanyo, please give him my love."

"If I see—" I broke off, staring at her.

She laughed, in that staccato way which I knew betokened strain in a Xuman.

"That was a slip, wasn't it? Well, if you are *half* with us, please don't report it, Tomass, to your superiors. Goodbye now."

It was then that I first realized that there really was

some kind of organized movement against us; and somehow, Kanyo was involved in it.

No, I wasn't going to report Psyl's "slip." But at last my feeble imagination began to work, and I saw what she had been driving at.

A liberal among conquistadors can afford to side with the natives only as long as the natives *are obviously on the losing side*. I had read a fair amount of Earth history, now, what was the parallel to our situation? We were a handful of aliens in a sea of Xumans. Like Clive in India, or like Cortés in Mexico. Could we be heading for an Indian Mutiny, a *noche triste*?

I shrugged the thought aside. No, not possible. Not even with the most ruthless coup could the Xumans do anything about *Riverhorse*. We had what Cortés and Clive had never had—an unsinkable gunboat in heaven. That star in its course would always fight for us—so I could afford to go on being a liberal, a Xuman-lover . . .

We flew to Xarth, with two landers.

The city was already being rebuilt, for Varan was taking his Princedom seriously, and he and Saimo had thrown themselves into the business of reconstruction with great energy (in spite of the heat—Xarth is nearly on the Equator). When I met them in their Palace, they were full of enthusiasm.

"It's not just the physical damage," said Varan, as we looked down from that rooftop over the battered city. "The Elders are capable of leading the people in that matter. But Saimo and I—we are trying to reconstruct the soul of Xarth. For a dozen dozen years now this state has been in the hands of warped leaders—kurar with an unhappy personal history. They are too ferocious, too male if you like. On the other hand, I've made it clear—we've made it clear—that we're not going to impose the Yelsai pattern on them. That would be madness—they would revolt if we tried it. Some things we have abolished—slavery, for instance—but Xarthians are going to remain a fierce, proud people. That is not necessarily bad—if the pride and the fierceness are properly channelled. If we have the time,

147

we will channel them. Tomass, I hope to hold the throne of Xarth until—until we both change," he said, looking at Saimo tenderly. "Since we are both the same age, it ought to happen about the same time. Then, if I have established enough goodwill here, I think the Xarthians may accept Saimo as their Prince—and Saimo will then be a kurar, which ought to satisfy the nobles. I suppose," he added, "it would be useful if we could see how they run things in the West Sector— Kanyo used to tell me how well those cities are governed—"

"You're going to have the chance to do just that," I told him; and while Belmondo looked on I explained that we wanted Saimo to come with us, and he too if possible.

He agreed at once, with a sardonic smile. "It seems this time the wind for once is blowing west to east. Well, let us be like balloon-traders."

Next day we flew from Xarth to Kvaryla, almost exactly along the Equator, one-third of the way round the planet. First we were following a canal, then we were over scorched red desert, then by late afternoon we saw the lush greenery of Lulam Ao, the "East Marsh." Here there were many intersecting canals and many cities close together: it was that part of the planet most like an Earthly tropical region. There were even some freshwater artificial lakes, and carefully grown strips of jungle.

Dave, Jack, and I were once more in the same medium ship, along with Varan. Saimo was travelling in the big lander with Belmondo and some marines and economic specialists. Belmondo had requested her presence because he wanted his troops to learn some Xuman during the flight, and we had to agree. Varan had not liked to part with her, even for this short while, but he could not see what harm she might come to. And at least, this arrangement gave us three a chance to talk to Varan—and vice versa. Jack and Dave were slowly learning Xuman, and we alternated language lessons with political conversation.

"I'm dead against the present setup," said Dave,

"and not only for your people's sake, Varan. It's psychologically corrupting to be an invader. You end up repressing not only the natives, but also half of yourself. Because half of yourself can't help but be on the natives' side."

"I just hate the way some of our guys behave," said Jack. "In Yelsai, in the streets, in that famous whorehouse, acting like they really were gods; even some of the girls, they get a terrific kick out of being waited on by Xuman servants—of course, they've never had servants before in their lives . . ."

"Sure, they're being corrupted," said Dave; "like I said, it's starting. It's not gone deep yet, but give it time . . . A few years should be enough."

"And on the other side, hatred is corrupting," said Varan. "We do not hate you star folk yet, but as you say, David, a few years will see it, if you take over many cities as you have already taken over some parts of Yelsai. And you have so many deadly weapons! Hatred and lasers are a bad combination. My teacher Kanyo used to tell me: 'There is one law that is universally true of weapons. If they exist and can be used, they will be.' Some day, my friends, some native will steal a laser, and learn to use it—that's not difficult—and then we will have shootings in city streets. That is the present you are storing up for those children your women are now carrying."

"Yeah," said Jack, when I had interpreted this. "I believe you, friend. I'd support any policy that would put an end to this situation—any policy barring violence, of course."

Varan looked from him to Dave and me; and said no more.

Kvaryla was an overwhelming city. It was four times as big as Yelsai, and ten times as rich—and felt twenty times as hot. I exaggerate, of course, but the place *was* a shock, even after Xarth. We put down on a lawn of the royal palace an hour before sunset, and the air engulfed us like a turkish bath—it was nearly 40° C, humidity 80 percent. This was their summer, of course—the locals said it would be a little cooler in winter and at night.

"Is the East Sector all like this?" groaned Belmondo.

The King of Kvaryla smiled ingratiatingly.

"Idaxir is a little hotter but a little drier. Idavaan is cooler in the summer because it is quite far north—but it is very cold in winter, much colder than Yelsai. Really, we have one of the best climates in the world here in Kvaryla—warm, moist, equable . . ."

Belmondo gave us all a look—a look which said "Cross off the East Sector." We all agreed—for people like us who had been living for years in an even 23° C, the East Sector would not do at all as a place for our first great colony.

That night the King showed us some of the attractions of Kvaryla, right on his palace roof garden: in fact, they danced for us. They were naked, bejewelled kynthi—all royal slaves. Belmondo eyed them with a flicker of interest, but they were no great improvement on the talent available in Yelsai—and it was still bloody hot. The First Officer declared he felt too limp for violent exercise that evening.

Varan and I talked to the King. It seemed that slavery was legal through most of the East Sector—but everywhere the slave had to be freed at least when he or she turned Elder.

"In Kvaryla only kynthi can be slaves," said the King virtuously. "In our enlightened city, they must be liberated as soon as they become kurar. But our girls are famous for their beauty, and if you buy them young you can keep them two dozen years. You like to go to the slave-girl market tomorrow? I will take you, make sure you get a good deal. Bidding begins at noon . . ."

"At *noon*!" groaned Belmondo, when I translated. "Oh, no! And who wants to buy up whores when we can hire 'em from the old Fire-fish? By noon—hell, by *dawn* tomorrow, we'll be on our way . . ."

And by dawn we were.

"And to think," said Jack, as we flew on, "that hell-hole was going to be our prize, if we persuaded Telesin to let us conquer the world for her."

"I have a suspicion," said Dave, "that we won't find any city significantly more attractive than Yelsai."

Thirty degrees east of Kvaryla, for the first time, we crossed an ancient coastline. Down sank the land, but we maintained our height, and from a long way up saw the dried sea bed of Laral Ao. Mostly it was white with salt deposits, but in places there were patches of ochre weed and even once or twice a streak of green.

"Tula," said Varan with a grin. "That gets everywhere."

"That must be one of the toughest plants on any planet," said Dave. "Do you know, my Rosa's been investigating the ones on the palace roof at Yelsai? She found they could stand heat, cold, electric shocks—she ran a wire right inside one tube, and sent a good strong current through—300 volts—and the plant wasn't harmed. Nor did the current leak—those rubbery stems are perfect insulators. Varan, your people really should use electricity more—you've got some excellent natural cable lying around, just made for—well, say, *telegraphy*."

"What is *telegraphy*?" asked Varan.

I explained.

"Yes, that is certainly a good idea," said the prince, with a ghost of a smile. "Perhaps the elders should take it up, and save themselves the mental strain of *telepathy*."

At last we crossed the opposite shoreline, and in about 20 degrees North latitude came down at the balloonport of the city of Xiriko, West Sector. It was nearly noon in high spring, and hot but not unbearable. The notables of Xiriko were there to receive us. They were mostly women, but the actual head of the state was a man—a man dressed in a light suit of blue linen. The top half of the suit was a loose tunic, and the lower half something like pajamas. The women were mostly dressed the same way, though a few wore skirts instead of pants. Altogether, the West Sector garb was curiously like our own Earthly costume. For one thing, none of these women exposed their breasts.

"Welcome to the Republic of Xiriko," said the man

in the blue suit. "I am President Getlin, and these are my Cabinet. Allow me to present . . ."

It was strange, very strange—because it wasn't strange enough. The breeziness, the casual efficiency, the lack of ceremonious bows or elaborate forms of address—all these were in strong contrast to the manners of the East Sector. President Getlin reminded me of a certain administrator I had known in Copernicus. It was like crossing twenty light years, and then meeting our doubles—red-skinned, six-fingered doubles, but doubles all the same. To add to the effect, the President had arranged accommodation for us not in a palace, but in a *hotel*.

"Not being a king, I don't have a palace—just my own little house," explained Getlin, as he showed us to our suite. "We don't go in for queens or kings much in West Sector. Only the city of Elthon has a queen, and she merely reigns without ruling. All the outer cities are republics, and we even have a loose federal organization, with a secretariat in Xulpona . . ."

It seemed that West Sector was less enthusiastic about excitement and *history* than most other parts of Xuma. They had not had any intra-Sector war for the past three-gross years.

Well, for the rest of that day we were given an official tour of Xiriko. The President himself showed us round the Assembly building, the museum, the library. I was struck by several points. First, these people had no problem about "perverts": the President himself was a kurar, and people of all four sex groups had equal political rights. Secondly, of course there was no slavery of any kind. Saimo and Varan were much impressed and asked the President many questions.

The third point hit me only after a while. It was when we were in the great City Library. Of course! Most of the Xumans in the library, including some of the librarians, were redskins, not grey-skinned elders.

"We do not think only elders should be intellectuals," said the President with a smile. "Even some of the *authors* on these shelves were sexed folk when they wrote."

At the end of the day, there was a brief conference

held in our hotel suite. The general feeling among Belmondo's party was that West Sector would *not* be a good place to establish a colony. The climate was as good as Yelsai's, but not better; and . . .

They had a hard job putting it into acceptable words; but I understood, all right. These people were too *like* us. They might not accept our dominance easily. As it was, the President and his cabinet were acting as though it did not exist.

"You'd think we were just a bunch of damn redskin tourists from the next damn redskin city," said Belmondo plaintively.

After Xiriko, we made one more short hop in West Sector before heading for Yelsai and home: we decided to visit the city of Xulpona. This was partly at my request—I was curious to see the home city of Psyl and Kanyo.

Xulpona turned out to be almost another Xiriko, except that the President here was a normal *kun* woman, a lady named Huy. When we arrived at the balloonport in the cool of the morning, Huy and her Cabinet were there to greet us. Belmondo swaggered a bit, and even briefly tried to impress Huy with some newly learned Xuman. Unfortunately, instead of saying Peral Xúl (West Sector), he kept saying Peral Xùl (Shit Sector)—which seemed to please Huy and her ladies, though possibly not in the way Belmondo intended. Our leader responded to the ladies' titters as though he had made a great hit: he became positively gallant. In his next sentence he went on to confuse *ula* (hole) and *yla* (city), and the result was uproarious . . .

Saimo, however, looked definitely upset during this conversation. I thought at the time that she was pained at these results of her teaching—I should have known better, for Angel had always laughed merrily when I made similar mistakes a month previously. Apparently Huy noticed something; for as we moved into the airport building, she said to Saimo:

"Travel does get wearing, my dear Princess; but we've fixed you a nice quiet hotel right close by here, overlooking West Park, just opposite the Library . . ."

I asked President Huy about Psyl and Kanyo. She had heard of them, all right.

"Fine people," she said. "Kanyo was a distinguished scholar even before he changed to Elder, an archaeologist, astronomer . . . We've got some books by him in that Library."

"Oh," I said, "on what subject?"

"Mainly archaeology—" she began; but then checked herself. "But I don't suppose such matters would interest you interstellar visitors, and anyway, you wouldn't be able to read our script, would you?"

Now in fact by this time I had taken some lessons, and *could* partly puzzle out Xuman writing; but on an impulse I thought it best not to admit that. I told the President that Kanyo was my friend, and for sentiment's sake I would just like to see some of his works.

"Well then," said Huy, "of course you can visit the Library . . ."

I did so alone, while the others were being shown round the city. And quickly the red-skinned librarian found me what I wanted—a manuscript book by Kanyo entitled *Some Observations on the Remains of the Divine Starship.*

I read that title over and over. Yes, it certainly said *that.* Then I opened the book. I could not read it fluently, but I spelled out enough to see that it seemed to be describing an actual wrecked or partly wrecked ship.

". . . tradition has it," I read on the third page, "that the good gods left it behind when they departed to the Great Center; left it perhaps to serve us little mortals in some hour of great need . . ." And then the writing became more difficult, as Kanyo obviously warmed up to his subject and dashed off his thoughts more quickly.

I returned to the main librarian's desk, but there I found that the red-skinned woman who had served me had disappeared. In her place was a grey-faced elder.

"This book," I said, "it describes a star-ship, doesn't it? Where is this ship to be found?"

The grey one burst into a light tenor laugh.

"Sir, that book is our respected Kanyo's one venture into fiction—*science fiction,* if I may coin a term. There is no such star-ship in existence—the only one in our system is your own, sir, and where that is you know better than I. In a sense, this is a remarkable book," he went on, taking it from my hands. "For many years now it has amused many readers—who never realized that it was prophetic. For Kanyo, let me tell you, imagines a ship rather like yours, though somewhat larger. He even endows it with a weapon something like—well, like whatever it was that you used on the city of Xarth. But, as is usual with *fictional* inventions, this one is much exaggerated. Kanyo mentions a destructive beam expanding to a diameter of several miles! Impossible, of course . . . luckily for all of us, may I say?"

He paused. "If you have finished with the book, sir, shall I return it to its shelf?"

His pause, his casualness—I say this with hindsight—they were timed just right. If that elder had acted differently—if he had betrayed greater tension—then possibly the whole history of Xuma might have been vastly different. I don't know: but I know that my *own* history would have been different . . .

I let him take that book from me, and I walked back to our hotel.

I found Dave and Jack in the room which had been reserved for the Prince and Princess of Xarth. At once I saw that I had come in on—well, a bit of a *scene*. Saimo was sitting on the low bed; Varan beside her was clasping her shoulders; Dave was hovering near the couple as though he would like to help but didn't know how; and Jack was standing by the door, looking worried. Saimo was gulping in that heart-rending way which was the Xuman equivalent of tears.

Jack turned to me at once. "Tom, we still don't know enough of the language—not when they speak fast, and Saimo's not talking English to us now. Can *you* find out what's the matter?"

"My dear friends," I said in Xuman, going forward, "what has happened?"

Varan looked up. "Nothing—nothing unusual," he said.

But I could see he was trembling with suppressed rage. I got an idea.

155

"It couldn't be—that these women of Xulpona have insulted Saimo? Surely they know that Mid-Sector has different traditions of dress . . ." For Saimo was dressed as usual in an elegant bare-fronted gown, which showed off her young breasts, her proud new womanhood—to my eyes, very beautifully.

Saimo turned her eyes to me. "Oh, Tomass, I should not have mentioned it! Now I will be the cause of trouble. But I do not want to go alone in that flier tomorrow."

"It was not the Xulpona women," said Varan, "it was your moonface *men.* During that last flight from Xiriko, Belmondo . . . I cannot say it. One of your soldiers was piloting, the flight was smooth, Belmondo did not have to keep his seat . . ."

"But surely," I gasped, "there were so many of them!"

"The others mostly did not interfere," said Varan. "Only one of the money-experts protested a little. But for him, I think that other one would have raped her. As it was, he behaved to her as though he were in the House of the Fire-fish, and she was one of the girls employed there. It seems he has been too many days separated from those delights . . ." He paused. "Saimo has acted intelligently, I may say. She has pretended—since—not to mind, to have forgotten. But I will not let her travel with those men again. I will say she is sick, that she must have quiet and less company, and I will take her place in the bigger flier. I know enough of your tongue now so that they can learn Xuman from *me.*"

I knelt and kissed Saimo on the forehead. She had stopped gulping now, and she smiled at me. "It is all right, Tomass," she said.

"No, dammit, it is *not* all right," I said in English, getting up and facing the others. Then I told them what had happened.

Jack swore. "The crude stupid bastard!"

Dave said: "Varan, please don't think we are all like that."

"I know you are not," said Varan, "but that does not alter the situation. What would you wish to do, Earthmen, if it were your case? If strangers from another world behaved so to your wives?"

There was a silence. Finally, Jack said, "I guess I'd go for them with a wrench. Or a laser."

"I am not going to be driven by my emotions," said Varan. "The situation is too serious for that. But, my friends, do you not see that, sooner or later, there may have to be a little fighting—perhaps even killing? We Xumans cannot merely *persuade* your Captain and Belmondo to stop treating us like slaves. Some violence there must be. I hope it will not frighten you into taking Belmondo's side."

"Damn right it won't," said Jack. "Belmondo deserves all he gets."

"Thank you," said Varan. "Do not fear for those you love. We know who are our friends among you moon-faces. Above all, we have no quarrel with your women."

"Glad to hear it," said Dave, tight-lipped.

Then there was a pause, and we relaxed. I had the feeling of crossing an invisible line. I thought now that Varan would speak of definite *plans*; but he did not, for which I was grateful.

"Well, one good thing," said Jack after a while, "we've only one more dry ocean to cross—and then tomorrow we'll be home to Yelsai." Dave nodded agreement.

"I have a suggestion to make," said Varan calmly, "about tomorrow's flight. Perhaps you should take a close look at one of our seabeds. There is an astronomical observatory in the West Ocean, just on the Equator and about halfway across from here to Yelsai. It is sited on a sort of island. Maybe you Earth folk should land there and inspect it."

"What a curious place for an observatory!" I said. "Why is it there?"

"I believe it was placed there very many years ago—when the relations between the Order and the city-states were not as stable as today. The Order wanted an observatory on the Equator mainly for solar observations, so they chose a site which no nation could claim. It is certainly an unpleasant place to live, that

157

Svityol—very hot when the sun is high. But the Order is very traditional, so the place is still manned. If we left very early tomorrow morning, you could land there before the heat becomes intolerable for you."

I looked at Varan, and wondered what his angle was. He smiled mockingly, and added:

"I say this lest the great Belmondo should suspect we are concealing things from him. The Svityol Observatory lies just on our route—he is sure to notice it. So I tell you all about it in advance."

"I get it," I nodded. "O.K., we'll tell the big boss, and see what he says."

We took off from Xulpona well before dawn. Under our ships the city showed up as an orderly array of delicately tinted jewels, for the phosphorescent street-lights were painted with dyes of various colors. We followed a pink avenue that led out of town towards the southeast, and then we were roaring over the dark countryside, with the first flush of dawn on our left and bright dwindling stars overhead.

Saimo sat quietly in one of the back seats next to Dave. Jack Willis acted as navigator, and I flew the ship. As the dawn grew brighter, I saw the rim of the dried ocean ahead of us; and simultaneously noticed a star crawling across the sky, down towards that low horizon.

All of us colonists had by now grown a bit blasé about the appearances and disappearances of *Riverhorse*, and we didn't do all that much radio-talking between planet and ship, but in these landers the radios were of course always kept switched on. I had been ignoring the faint hiss of static ever since we had taken off. Suddenly it erupted into a voice.

"Captain Mannheim, calling all surface parties. I repeat, Mannheim to all surface parties. For your information. We have just picked up a message on the Solar aerial, and processed it. I think it is best you hear the playback as of now, so, stand by. Here it is. You will realize, of course, that in our time it is twenty decimal nine years old."

Then there was an outburst of scratchy noises, and fi-

nally a quiet, almost ghostly voice. It took me a couple
of seconds to realize—of course, it was not a real human voice from the Moon, but our own robot-voicer
from *Riverhorse* re-articulating the interstellar signal.
The Ghost, as we called him/it, spoke clear English
words, but without the slightest emotional inflection.

"Lunaris Hills Base to Riverhorse . . . We advise
that preparations for Riverboat Two and Riverhorse
Two are suspended for duration of present emergency
and indefinitely thereafter . . . Decision has been taken
by Euram Strategic Command in light of present serious situation . . . Commander of Riverhorse One is requested to take full initiative for colonization of any
habitable planet or planets of 82 Eridani system without relying on reinforcements . . ."

"What the hell?" yelled Jack almost in my ear.
"What's this *emergency*?"

As if in answer, the Ghost resumed.

"For details of emergency situation here see previous message of 9/12/2122 . . . This message ends . . ."

Mannheim's voice cut in. "Before you jam the wires,
troops, let me say, we didn't receive that previous
message. We had a slight fault here yesterday with the
Solar antenna, which we have now fixed. I guess we'll
have to use our imaginations till we hear from Lunaris
again."

"If we hear from Lunaris again," whispered Dave behind me. "Oh my god. Oh my god."

Well, Mannheim now gave us all a pep talk, saying
that nothing that might have happened on the Moon
really altered our situation. Star colonists really *were* on
their own from the start, period. *Riverboat II* had been
a projected backup ship for Epsilon Eridani, and *Riverhorse II* a backup for us: but even if both these proj-
ects had gone ahead with full priority they couldn't
have helped us within the next 25 years.

"As of now, we just have to remember—the future
of the human race on Ares—perhaps in the whole universe—depends on us and on our womenfolk. We will
not fail; with God's help, we shall overcome. God bless
our country, Euram-Moon; God bless you all—"

The next moment, the tiny star that was Riverhorse

One-and-Only disappeared on the blood-red horizon.

Saimo said quietly: "Tomass, what is Euram Strategic Command?"

"Our generals," I said. "They're supposed to take over if our civilian government on the Moon are put out of action. I guess that is what has happened."

Dave kept on saying "Oh my god—oh my god." For a psych boy, I thought he took it rather badly.

"Three years," muttered Jack, "three years—2119 to 2122. We beat it out of Doomsday by three little years . . ."

The observatory was a green pimple on the pale, bleached seabed, and as we jetted up closer the pimple became a molehill, then a mountain. Over on the right a long green streak was a line of tula plants stretching out from Svityol southwards—as I guessed, heading for the nearest city on the south shore of the ocean, which was Dlusar, from which a canal (and more tula plants) led straight to Khadan. Down both slopes of the Svityol hill, north and south, there also stretched several miles of netting supported on poles—the kind of netting that was used to catch trade balloons as they moved on their inevitably east-to-west courses; and in fact there were a couple of golas moored against the net. Obviously Svityol was quite a going concern. It was a curiously steep little mountain, with buildings near the summit and a small black circular crater at the very top.

"That is the great telescope," said Saimo; "it is sunk vertically into the hill, and the sun's rays are reflected into it by mirrors. Or so Varan says Kanyo taught him."

"Telescope?" I said. "Reminds me of the pipe of a volcano—or Jules Verne's mighty space cannon for the first-ever moon shot. Hey, that tube must be *huge*! As big as our superscopes on Farside—if we still have superscopes on Farside."

I thought there was a good chance that Belmondo would not now want to land at Svityol, but no: over the intercom he said it was our duty to be thorough in our investigations of native technology, especially in the light of what we had just heard . . .

So down we went. We landed on a small plateau just below the observatory buildings.

Boy, was that place hot! When we got out of the landers, it was already over 30 Celsius and climbing—and the sun had been up only an hour. In the old days, when the oceans were oceans, Svityol hill must have been a sea mount, not a true island, for we were well below shore level—but surely a very young sea mount, for waves should have eroded such an abrupt shape . . . The hot air here was *thick*. If it hadn't been so dry—less than 25 percent humidity—it would have been intolerable. As it was, we hated every minute we were there. For a really long stay in Svityol, humans would need space suits with cooling systems, and we hadn't brought any along on this trip.

As we stepped out of the landers, a small group of elders detached themselves from the shade of the observatory buildings. In a moment or two, as my eyes got used to the pitiless sunlight, I recognized the leading figure. It was Kanyo.

"Welcome to Svityol," said Kanyo, smiling. "Ah, how nice to see so many old friends! My dear pupil Varan—and you, Tomass Carson . . ."

"Psyl asked me to give you her love," I said. "But I thought you had gone to Khadan."

"There was a change of plan—at least, I suppose so. The Supreme Court of Poetry does not always inform us why they wish us to go to certain places. Some of us elders think Svityol is a punishment posting! But I flatter myself that I was sent here because of my astronomical qualifications. There is a program going on here on the analysis of sunlight as it is filtered through the lesser particles of the Ring Belt. But come in now, out of the heat, and we will show you everything . . ."

We trotted round through various minor rooms looking at small telescopes and spectroscopes, and the morning wore on. Varan once walked aside with Kanyo while other Elders showed us the instruments—but this seemed only natural: the former master and pupil would have much to say to each other. Belmondo began to sweat.

"Say, can't we cut this short?" he grunted. "Let's

have a look at Big Bertha, or whatever it is—the super-scope—and then hit the trail for home. This is a real hell-hole."

I told Kanyo. He smiled. "Very well. But I'm afraid it will be still hotter there. Let us go quickly."

In the end, Belmondo chickened out. In fact, he delegated the job to Jack and myself. Varan and Saimo remained with the other visitors, and Kanyo led Jack and me up to the lip of the crater. Below us lay a yawning black hole, a vast tube with a metal lip apparently leading into the bowels of the planet. Over the huge muzzle stood a spider's web of slim metal rods bearing inadequate-looking mirrors.

"Looks like a new rig," commented Jack, regarding the framework.

"Yes," said Kanyo casually, "we had to refurbish it lately. The observing room is underground. This way, please."

We went down a nearby shaft, spiral stairs leading into semi-gloom relieved by star-worm lamps. This shaft was definitely not new—at one turning of the staircase I saw a brief phrase carved in the stone of the wall-slabs: *xutan xar*. The letters were in an old style of noncursive, and the words meant "Excavation Four."

"You know," I said, as we went on down, "this is one hell of a telescope you've got here, Kanyo. When was it built?"

"Oh, millions of years ago," said Kanyo lightly. "Actually, it has been rather neglected for a long time. One of my duties here is to restore it to full working order. I am applying some newly developed ideas to its operation."

"Photographs?" said Jack. "I know you know that principle. You should get some fine shots with that enormous aperture."

"I think it possible we may," said Kanyo gently.

Then we had reached the control room. It was a clean room, brightly lit with phosphorescent globes, and it was fairly full of apparatus and several elders stooping over the gadgets. I know a little about astronomy, of course—who doesn't—but I am no expert on big scopes, and neither was Jack. The whole place looked pretty mysterious to both of us.

"What's this?" Jack kept saying; or "what the hell's this?"

One thing we realized at once was that much of the apparatus was electrical—and these items were all new. There was a control desk, properly wired up, with buttons, dials and things like—well, a bit like gunsights. Kanyo told us those were finders for the big scope.

"How about power?" asked Jack.

"Solar cells," explained Kanyo. "We *have* got as far as that, you know. And we have plenty of sunlight here! Not that we need very much power for our purposes. The moving parts are well balanced, we merely have to trigger them, so to speak."

"O.K.," said Jack, "so when do we get a look through the big tube?"

"You *don't*," said Kanyo sharply. "The first rule in solar astronomy is, never, never look with your own eyes at the sun. For us, the sun is a symbol of truth; but too much truth can be blinding. Deadly."

And then we had had enough. On our way up, I told Kanyo about my experience in the Library of Xulpona.

"I really didn't know you wrote science fiction," I said, laughing. "We ought to found a fan club, us two. But I never guessed you would write such stuff, Kanyo."

Kanyo looked at me sharply. "I don't. Not any more, anyway. Life is too serious to be dealt with by fictional methods, Tomass."

Chapter Eleven

By the end of Second Month '0-8-5—that is, late southern autumn—all we moonfaces had decided where our first colony on Xuma must be.

Yelsai.

The City of Six Gates held so many attractions for us. Inside the walls, it was bustling with cheerful native life—cafés, markets and those famous pleasure houses. Beyond the walls, there was a twenty-mile-wide district of minor canals and greenness before the major canals began to thread their lonely way through the red deserts, like an Egyptian Delta leading to three Niles. It became quite the thing, for some of us, to go picnicking in this *lulenthi* (oasis) area, and the S/Vs roared along the formerly quiet stone-paved roads—especially the road to Ylaxul. Ylaxul, twenty miles west of Yelsai, had been a seaport on the edge of the Western Ocean when the Western Ocean held water. In the Great Disaster it had been destroyed; but over two million years it had been lovingly restored by the Elders. Now many of its palaces and towers stood in romantic loneliness on the edge of that empty bay—a sacred spot, to which the people of Yelsai used to make pilgrimage, always on foot, to meditate on the mystery of Time. Our folk made the pilgrimage always by S/V—astro-landers would have been quicker, but S/Vs were cheaper on fuel, and we were already facing a problem about that. Soon we would have to restructure local industry to keep ourselves in supplies . . . and while we were about that, there was a popular suggestion that Ylaxul ought to be *developed*. The natives should be urged to build cafés there, and put up hamlor-meat stalls; and a small canal or at least a pipeline might be built, to feed swimming pools . . . Why, the place had definite possibilities; we could soon make it as lively and attractive as Lunaris Lido.

We did send out a few other air expeditions to other parts of the planet, but the verdict was always the same: there was no other area of Xuma clearly better than this; and we liked the Yelsaians, and they seemed to like us and treated us with sufficient respect. The climate was not bad, either. It was cold at night now, but we had efficient native fur robes and tula-lined jackets, and the skies by day were a glorious deep blue and the noon warmth was enough to melt the night ice on the canals. We did not see any reason to move, and we were certainly not going to spread ourselves thinly over the face of the planet. There really could be no danger from the natives, of course—not with our unsinkable gunboat coming round every four hours—but some feelings can't be reasoned away. On this new extra-solar continent, Yelsai was our Jamestown, our Plymouth: our new home.

It was a minor snag that it wasn't, officially, ours—that it was the capital of our ally, Queen Telesin, and in it we had only the status of allies, of strangers within the gates.

We held meetings about that. At one important conference in the balloonport Fort, Dave Weiser and I recommended strongly that we do nothing to upset the status quo.

"What's in a name?" said Dave. "We can have all we want here, we can be secure and watch our children grow. The Queen and her Ladies have voted us permanent subsidies—two gold sulans a day for every man-jack and woman-jill of us in gratitude for our aid in the Xarth war, so what more do we need? Yelsai is our colony already in *fact*; why bother with titles?"

Well, we nearly swung the meeting. Nearly, but not quite. Maybe I spoilt things by citing a historical parallel—the British imperialists in India. For a long time the British pretended to be only "allies" of the local emperors, while hogging the wealth of the country. I guess the American tradition is too strong in Euramians: our guys couldn't be imperialists in the old cynical mould—they liked things legal, above board, and—*democratic*.

So we were going to be citizens of Yelsai. Great!—but we were badly out-numbered by the existing citizens, so we would have to be even more citizenish than the redskins. What we would do was, rig the constitution. In any case the constitution needed altering; Varan had unsettled the Young Guards, and they were now muttering that it was wrong that the Twelve Ladies should have all the power apart from the Queen. O.K., so we'd have males eligible for the Queen's Council—and immediately we'd pack the board with twelve *Earth* males and three Earth females.

I forget now just how they made this proposal out to sound fair or democratic, but they did. Something about "provisional representation," or "guided democracy." We, with our great experience of democratic constitutions—all of two-and-a-half centuries—would have special powers to lead this two-and-a-half-million-year-old people.

Belmondo still hadn't learned more than a few set phrases of the language, so he used me as interpreter when he informed the Queen about the Great Gerrymander. Telesin was magnificent. She had been looking almost frail these past few weeks, but she now drew herself up to her full height—about the height of my nose—and said:

"Tomass, tell your leader that we will submit, since we have no choice. But may I ask why you are doing this to *us*, when we are your friends, and it is Xarth that you conquered?"

"It's too hot in Xarth," I said.

The day after that, Telesin fell ill.

At least, that's what I thought it was. But halfway through that morning, Sally came to our apartment on the palace roof, and said:

"Tom, she's fading."

"*What?* You mean she's *dying*?"

"No, *fading*. Her skin is turning grey. There are yellow streaks in her hair. It takes a few weeks, but after that—poor Telesin will have no more sex. She won't be a woman, she'll be an *Elder*, like—like Psyl."

"O my god!" I said, staring. "What have we done to her?"

"Nothing," said Sally, "this is one thing you can't blame us for. She knew it was nearly time. Tom, in our terms she's *fifty-three*."

Fifty-three! I could have known, but I had never worked it out. When I had first met her, Telesin had struck me as young, or ageless, young at heart, as though like Cleopatra age could not wither her . . . but now age had. I stammered:

"Can I see her? I—"

"No, she doesn't want that," said Sally. "She told me specially, she didn't want to see any of her former lovers. Not till it was all over."

"Her former—" I began.

Sally's mouth twitched. Then she burst out into a laugh—not a very mirthful laugh. "Oh, hell, Tom, I knew about that long ago. I've been friends with Telesin for some time . . . Tom Carson, the great space hero, the first Earthman to lay an alien bird, and all that—"

Well, we had a bit of a—let me call it an explanation. After a while, when we were feeling a bit more cheerful, Sally said:

"I wonder who will be the next Queen? Or will Belmondo and his gang decide that Queens aren't *democratic*?"

I don't think Sally or I would have guessed in a million years the solution that the new (packed) Council decided upon. It seems our guys were rather taken with the idea of a Queen—especially a queen who was basically a *beauty* queen, selected by a panel of males. What did they do? They decided to hold the election—

the contest, or whatever you like to call it—more or less as before; but this time they packed the electors' panel, too, with a majority of *Earth* men, and they made *Earth* women eligible for the Queenship.

Oh, they didn't actually hold a beauty parade, with red- and white-skinned birds parading up and down in bathing suits. That might have been fun, but Belmondo's henchmen felt it might also be lacking in dignity—they didn't want to lower the dignity at least of the *Earth* girls. And anyway, that wasn't the local custom, either, because the really famous beauties of Yelsai were well known to the young men (mostly guardsmen) of the panel, same as film stars used to be in the old days of the Solar System. And, like film stars, I might add that Queens were not chosen merely for good looks—personality counted too.

Yes, and I'm sure it did on this occasion. Because that panel—two-thirds colonists and one-third redskin boys—they went into a huddle and announced that the next Queen of Yelsai would be—*Sally Carson.*

I was with Sally in a sort of common-room we then had in the middle of the palace penthouse, when the news was announced. Dave and Rosa were there, and Jack's wife Sheila and several other colonists, when Jack came bursting in and told us. At first I thought he was kidding, and so did Sally.

"No, seriously, folks," he said. "You know I was on the board—well, it'll be on the intercom any minute now. Fact is, Sal, all the red boys voted solidly for you, and several of us white men did too, so you had it made. Long live Queen Sally the First of Yelsai!"

Everyone cheered; and then the announcement did come on, and it was true. Sally went almost as red as a Xuman. She felt she was being got at in some way, and she wanted to refuse the honor—if it was an honor; but I said, "Let's discuss this in private." When we were back in our room, I put it to her.

"Look, Sal, I don't know why those red boys did it—maybe they *do* think you're pretty, or maybe they like the way you've done what you could for Saimo and Telesin and so on—but I think we should go along with this. As the Xuman proverb has it, go with the wind. Maybe, for what the position's worth, you can use it to counter Belmondo's gang."

Sally's lip trembled, and her blue eyes were bright. "I must see Telesin about this," she said. "She's almost through her Change now, and she *will* see *me*."

Well, the upshot of that interview was that Telesin convinced Sally to accept the—the crown of Yelsai.

"She believes the boys are not mocking me at all," said Sally seriously. "They do genuinely like me, and they think I can do some good. And Telesin expects to be up in time for Midwinter Feast, and then she will crown me with her own hands. That is customary—the outgoing Queen crowns the incoming one."

"What am I going to be—the King?" I asked.

Sally laughed. "No: you have no particular status. Your courtesy title is *Xylir kunaya*—"

"Royal *lover*. Great!"

"And," said Sally, "according to local law and custom I have every right to take a *second* husband—not to mention any number of *unofficial* lovers. How about that?"

Midwinter in Yelsai—it's rather a curious festival, even without a Coronation thrown in. It falls on the last night of Third Month, since the Xuman year begins at the northern spring equinox; but the people of Yelsai have also a local year system which differs from the planetary one—they count by "sun seasons," from midwinter to midwinter. So Midwinter '0-8-5 was also New Year's for the Yelsai sun season '0-8-5 to '0-8-6. People would be wearing their best furs and tula-lined robes—even the naked *vep* would sport quilted cloaks during the cold of the evening parties—and the citizens would give each other presents, and wish each other Happy New Sun, *suhaiti tlavol*. And this year, with the Coronation thrown in, it would be an extra-special festival.

It certainly was—but I'll come to that later.

By Midwinter, Varan and Saimo had been in Xarth for a month or so, but when they heard of Telesin's Change, they made it back to Yelsai. They came by balloon, with a small escort of Xarthian nobles and guardsmen, and landed on the canal just north of the city—peacefully, this time—and marched with their men to Yel Karagor, the Gate of Dragons. Here Varan quartered his Xarthians—tactfully outside the gate, in a house near the balloonport—and came on in to visit us in the Palace.

We met a day or two before the Festival, in Telesin's new chamber. She had moved to the monastery block under the Astronomy Tower, and her apartment was next to Psyl's. Psyl was there too, and she was holding Telesin's hand when Sally and I entered.

It gave me a deep shock to see those two grey people, hand in hand. Telesin still had fine features, but they were sharper. She had not yet cut her hair, but her former sleek black glossy glory was now the color of dried straw, and her skin, once so smooth, so supple and so red, was now a dull rough grey. She still wore the crown of Yelsai with its pendant jewels, but she wore it above the white robe of an Elder.

I tried to speak, and could not. Then she spoke, in a voice musical enough, but quite different from the womanly honeyed tones I remembered so well—it was a cool tenor voice, like that of a metal bell chiming in a cave of ice.

"Tomass," she said, "do not grieve. One must go with the wind, even the wind of time." She smiled faintly, coolly. "I know it seems worse to you moon-faces, because you are always fixed in your sex—to lose that, you think it is like losing your self. But remember, I have been without sex before, and after that I was a man. I knew *this* was coming within the year, even when I first met you, Tomass." Her smile became more lively, almost mischievous. "I am glad it did not come three months earlier, however! Sally, my friend, you need not be jealous of me now—but my memories of that time will be happy ones."

I almost blushed. "I—I was so stupid . . ."

Her laughter tinkled like glockenspiel. "Yes, you were a bit, my dear *god*—but it is I who should be ashamed for seducing you over that Water of Dreams and prying out your secrets. However, my motives were not *merely* political, and it seems no great harm has come of it, and Sally has forgiven me. Now, Tomass, I hope we can be simply friends."

Varan said: "Mother, what will you do—after the Festival?"

"I will go to Khadan," said Telesin.

"That is customary," explained Psyl. "Former queens of Yelsai always make the Pilgrimage. There is much that Telesin should learn in Khadan—perhaps lessons that I myself never learned properly."

"How can you take it—this—so calmly?" I blurted out. "Telesin, I—"

"There is no other proper way to take it," said Psyl. "Tomass, one does not lose what one has never really possessed. Man, woman, even individual being—these are only games, roles we have been playing. That is easier for us to see than for you, because you do not play so many roles."

"Life's *not* just a game," I protested. "*Kanyo* doesn't think so, anyway. Last time I saw him, he said life was serious."

"So it is," said Varan, with the ghost of a smile. "But then, a game can be serious too."

"This is all too deep for me," said Sally lightly. "Say, Telesin, I hope you won't stay permanently in Khadan. I could do with your advice when I'm Queen . . . you will come back, won't you?"

"Perhaps," said Telesin. "It may depend on what happens. In Yelsai; also in Khadan." She smiled. "Well, one good thing—it will be nice for me to see Aoak again."

"Again?" I murmured.

"Yes, Tomass, again—I knew him very well indeed at one time . . ."

"Aoak was my father," said Varan abruptly. "It was he who inspired me with respect for so-called perverts."

I looked my amazement; and Telesin laughed.

"Aoak was indeed a person to inspire respect. He was good at everything, that one! Including love-making . . . As a kynthi, the darling of the army; as a kurar captain, a fine leader of soldiers, and later a very efficient manager of me and of the Fire-fish girls . . . And now I hear he is a superb scholar, an austere ascetic, and the wisest of the Supreme Ones in Khadan. There, you see how well it is possible to play the Great Game . . ."

"I suspect he is now playing a little game within the big one," I said, "and maybe Kanyo is one of his pieces?"

The Xumans went quiet. Clearly I had said the wrong thing—or too nearly the *right* thing.

"I wish you'd all confide in me," I said, irritated. "We've been going on like this for months now; and yet I might even be able to help you . . ."

Sally said brightly: "Telesin, hadn't we better go over the details of the Coronation again?"

Midwinter Evening was cold, but as usual fine and clear.

Just before sunset, Telesin crowned Sally in the great square before the Palace, taking that beautiful gold circlet and its pendants off her own head to do so. From yellow hair to yellow hair . . . And all the vast crowd of red-skinned people gathered in that place cried out *Psu Kunaya Sali,* Long Live Queen Sally.

Telesin said: "Wait, my dear, let me turn the circle a little . . ." And she arranged the crown so that the blue jewels were over Sally's forehead. "To match your eyes," smiled Telesin.

Sally's eyes were a very dark blue in that light, but they held a sparkle which I think might have been due to tears. She made a short, halting speech in quite good Xuman.

"I am ashamed," she said. "I am afraid that I do not deserve to be Queen of Yelsai. I will be Queen only as long as I believe the people of Yelsai wish it. And I will do my best to serve all you people, whether I wear this crown or do not wear it. Thank you all."

"That was well spoken by your wife," said Varan afterwards.

We were standing on the roof of the palace, for that was where the royal celebration was being held, in spite of the cold. There were little charcoal braziers between the tables of the roof garden, and red-skinned servants

were carrying round jugs of heated wine to the Queen's
guests. The Queen's guests were both Xumans and Earth
folk, about half-and-half—which meant, of course, that
the Xumans were grossly under-represented; but Sally
had done the best she could. The Queen's guests at least
appeared to be happy.

It was hard to remember that *the Queen* now meant
Sally.

She came out now from the Royal Apartments onto
the roof, and the jewels of her crown flashed in the
light of Dinu, the little moon. In the group with her
were the Twelve Ladies of Yelsai, and Saimo, and
Telesin—Telesin now with her hair cut short, like any
other sexless Elder. Sally and her friends took their
seats to watch a traditional Midwinter dance—a fertil-
ity dance by a troupe of *kurar* from the House of the
Fire-fish reinforced by a squad of handsome young
palace guardsmen. The dancers must have been in-
flamed with zeal—or something—because they were
really wearing very little—just brief loin-cloths and a
few straps.

Some of the fur-wrapped Earth women watching that
dance cheered and groaned and pretended to writhe
with frustration. Well, I'm not sure it was pretence, at
that. These were mostly women whose boyfriends were
"engineer" space-marines; they knew their menfolk
were using Xuman girls (almost every night, in some
cases), and because of the facts of anatomy there was
very little they could do by way of revenge.

I grinned and said to Varan, "Did you hear about
Belmondo's woman? She got so mad the other day, she
took some color stuff and stained her skin a nice brick
red, and went down to the Fire-fish and squared the
management. Then she put on an open-fronted Yelsai
gown—and offered herself for the usual fee to any customers that turned up. The Xuman men guessed at
once, of course, even though her hair *is* black; and they
left her alone. But half a dozen of our boys thought she
was terrific . . . They were too drunk to notice her ears
or the number of her fingers, or the fact that she had a
navel. She boasted about it afterwards, though, and she
and Belmondo have split up."

"Where is Belmondo now?" asked Varan soberly. He did not seem in a very party mood.

"He left here," I said. "Took the S/V and went off with some of his crowd to the balloonport. They're having another party there, you know—a *stag party*. That means, only men. Well, that's what they *say*. Actually, I believe they have hired some Fire-fish girls to entertain them there. The Earth girls are all here, I think."

"All but four who are in *Riverhorse*," said Varan, "and those are women of the gunners up there. Yes, I checked on that. Mannheim, now: he seems to be relaxing his rules, doesn't he?"

"Oh, maybe," I said.

Mannheim was among the revellers on the roof; he sat not far from Sally, in expectation of another dance number. He had come in from orbit in a medium lander which was parked farther down the roof in the wrecked area. The crew of the lander were all out of it, and most of them seemed to be hitting the wine. But it only needs one man to fly those machines, and the pilot was staying sober.

I looked up, and saw *Riverhorse* crawling up the western sky amid the faint glimmers of the Ring. There could not be many crew members aboard now—only the indispensable marines at their laser cannon; and four girls. Maybe they would be throwing a party, too.

Varan said to me, "Tomass, if there were no *Riverhorse*, what would you do?"

"Eh?" I said. "What is this, a joke?"

"Let us call it an intellectual game," he replied. "Kanyo used to put such problems to me, they are mental exercises we Xumans go in for—suppose one thing, then what is the best strategy to operate? They are teaching devices. Now, suppose there were no *Riverhorse*. What would happen to you Earth folk on Xuma?"

"I'd hate to think," I said. "If the *Horse* met with an accident—say, got hit by an asteroid or something—then I'm afraid our guys would get panicky, violent. We have an awful lot of firepower even on the ground, you know. All those landers and the S/Vs with their laser-cannon, and the sidearms . . . But we wouldn't be secure any more. We'd be afraid of being jumped—you

can always jump a guy at certain times, like when he's
drunk, asleep, or—"

"Or with a woman," said Varan. "Quite so, Tomass.
Then what?"

"Then we'd get trigger-happy. It would be horrible. I
wouldn't want any part of it. The racial problem is bad
enough as it is—"

"It is not a racial problem, it is merely a problem of
weapons," said the boy. "Kanyo is right: weapons will
always be used. The only way to save the situation
would be to destroy the weapons. Then it is true you
Earth folk would be reduced to equality with us, but
that would be better than the alternative. It is *always*
weapons that have been the problem, Tomass. I know
what has probably happened to your people on the
Moon—there has been no further word from them, has
there?"

"No."

"Well, now you have a chance—not on your Moon,
but here on Xuma. If you could destroy *all* the
weapons of mass destruction that Earthmen have
brought here, in one blow, and with very little loss of
life—would you do it? You, Tom Carson? *Would you
help me do it?*"

I felt my heart thumping. This didn't sound like an
intellectual game—it sounded like an approach. A
temptation to real treachery—or real heroism. And—
and I was not a hero.

I gave a sickly laugh. "Well, put it like that—if all
the guns were in one heap, and we could blast them—
yes, maybe I would. But this is all rubbish, Varan.
There *is* a *Riverhorse* . . ."

Somehow, it sounded funny—like saying "There *is* a
Santa Claus." But *Horse* was more real than Santa
Claus—there it was up in the sky—crawling east . . .

Suddenly Psyl was at our side, her grey face silver in
the moonlight. She said, more to Varan than to me:

"If it ever happens, it will happen soon."

"The tula has spoken?"

"Yes," said Psyl. "The word was *Great Center.*"

In the background I could hear the sounds of the
dancers re-assembling. It was to be a sword-dance of

the young guardsmen, a symbolic driving away of demons for the new sun season. But Sally and Telesin and Saimo were drifting over to us.

"No, you should tell him now," I heard Telesin say. "*You* must know, Sally, if it is sure."

"O.K. then," said Sally. "Tom, darling—I'm pretty sure I'm going to have a baby."

"Terrific," I said, kissing her.

"You don't sound terribly thrilled," said Sally.

"I am, really," I said. "It's what we've been hoping for, isn't it? I was just wondering what sort of life our children will have on this planet."

"Oh," said Sally, "the other couples who've started babies are pretty cheerful about that. Once Belmondo and Co. have been cured of their ridiculous suspiciousness, we're all going to live like lords. Literally, I mean. We are going to be the aristocrats of Yelsai, with country houses down on those beautiful canals, and town houses in town, and lots of red-skinned servants . . . Hey, Tom, aren't you listening?"

I wasn't listening, no. I had been staring at the sky, and now I was blinking my eyes, and trying to see something that wasn't there.

One moment *Riverhorse* had been crawling high in the west. I had looked away for a second, and now that I looked back—nothing.

"Hey," I said. "Hey, Psyl—has it gone into eclipse?"

"*Look at the shadow on the Belt!*" said Psyl, in a sort of a strangled whisper.

Then I realized that the starship could not have entered normal eclipse—it was still well before midnight, and the glimmering Ring extended past the zenith and halfway down the eastern sky to the line where it vanished into the shadow of the planet. *Riverhorse* had winked out halfway up the *western* sky, where the Ring was all bright—

—No, it wasn't, though! Right up through the Ring there was a thin line like a spear of darkness, a spear that was distorting even as I watched, the lower portion moving east more quickly than the upper, the thin bar of black becoming a curve. Of course, the lower portions were in quicker orbits . . . the lower portions of *what*? Of nothingness, of a gap in the whirling bits of Ring—a gap that had swallowed *Riverhorse* . . .

"Kanyo got a perfect shot, I think," said Varan. "Psyl, will you take the ladies away from here? Indoors is best. Tom and I have work to do."

They went, all of them; Sally seemed bewildered, but she made no protest. I was saying to myself, over and over, No, it can't be. I was lying—that was only the top of my mind gabbling. Underneath, I was seeing a picture—an absurdly steep little mountain with a black round hole in its top. The muzzle of a telescope. Telescope? I had already mentally compared it to Verne's space *gun*. Maybe, deep down, I had always known. Deep down, I was a traitor.

Varan was talking. "Tom, now do you understand? Now, there is no longer any *Riverhorse*. What you just saw was no illusion. See, the wake of the shot is still there. It is miles wide—a weapon of the gods, you understand, so powerful that all your laser cannon are nearly insignificant beside it. It was left behind two and a half million years ago in a half-wrecked god ship—a ship standing vertical, buried by our ancestors two million years ago and rediscovered later. Kanyo once wrote a treatise to explain how the weapon could be made to work again. Therefore he was sent by my father to Svityol, and for months now he has been striving to turn theory into practice . . . but that's enough for now. Now, Tom, there is no time to lose. Will you help us? If you will not, I think we will still win, but it may be bloody. And first I would have to silence—you."

I wasn't wearing a laser, and he wasn't wearing any weapon—yet he talked like that. If it came to it, I guessed he *could* silence me—with his bare hands.

"What do you plan to do?" I said hoarsely.

"Take that flying craft," he said, nodding at the lander. "And at once. It will not be long before someone in the Fort learns about *Riverhorse*."

"Hey, you can't fly that *and* shoot—"

"I might just manage. Flying on auto, I could use the gun. I would probably crash, but that might not matter.

177

But it would be desperate. I really need you, too, To-mass."

"Okay," I said, "tell me what to do." I didn't feel heroic at that moment—I felt trapped, desperate. But the chips were down now, and I wasn't in real doubt which side I was on, and on both sides there would be danger.

"Call that pilot over to the shrubbery that way. Pretend to have something secret to discuss. He's not a friend of yours, is he?"

"No. Quite the contrary."

"Good. That makes it easier."

Well, I did call the pilot over. He came, casting one look over his shoulder to where Mannheim had an arm round a Xuman Council-Lady, and another look at the door of the lander, which was ajar.

"Whad'ya want, Carson?" he said.

That was my worse moment in the whole operation, I guess. The next second a couple of red figures leapt out from behind a tula trunk. One clapped a hand over the pilot's mouth, the other ran him through with a sword.

"Come," cried Varan, running towards the lander.

All over that roof, sudden swift treachery was erupting. The few Earthmen who had worn lasers to the feast were being seized by Xuman guardsmen or soberly efficient Ladies. Nobody actually managed to draw a laser, though Mannheim tried: a young red-skinned sword dancer got him first with his sword. The Earth women were screaming, but I guessed they would be all right. I saw young guardsmen holding some of them carefully but firmly by the arms. Then I jumped into the lander after Varan.

"You fly," said Varan, diving for the seat by the gun.

"To the airport?" I said, as we rose from the roof.

"Yes. If we are lucky, all the S/Vs and the other landers will be parked outside the Fort, and the crews will be *in*side. The Fire-fish girls have orders from us—to keep the Earthmen happy . . . I will try to destroy all the vehicles. My Xarthians are lurking round the back of the building. They may have to go in, but I have asked them to kill as few as possible . ɪ ."

We got to the Fort just in time, I guess.

I made one run, nice and low, and Varan opened fire—and blew every one of the other landers into little pieces. Fuel erupted in bright flames . . . The noise on the ground must have been terrific. It must have been enough to shatter the party atmosphere in the Fort.

For when I came back for my second run, there were figures leaping over the area between the building and the S/Vs. Other figures were milling about nearer the building. There was enough light from the burning landers to see that the guys near the building were red-skins, those near the S/Vs Earthmen.

I gritted my teeth, and flew on steadily. Varan beat Belmondo's men to the draw—he got all the S/Vs, one of them with a guy already inside. More flames.

"Back again, please," said Varan. "We must finish this cleanly."

"Cleanly," I said. "Sure."

There were a couple of Earthmen still in the open: they had lasered all the Xarthians in sight. But on my third run, Varan lasered *them*.

"Land now, Tomass," he said.

I did, and he got out, and stood where the flickering light fell on him. I was manning the gun now, covering him more or less, but if anyone had fired from that building they would have got him for sure. But no one did.

Seconds later, a small figure ran out of the building, and knelt at Varan's feet. The girls from the House of the Spring Fire-fish seemed to have won the battle inside.

"We have a little more to do," said Varan, coming back to the lander. "The girls will bring us all the hand-lasers from the Fort—and then we must fly back to the Palace."

As the girls came out with the guns, I asked Varan about casualties.

"Not too bad, really. Belmondo and three men I lasered out here. One other the girls had to kill, and two the Xarthians did. My poor Xarthians! They lost half their number; and five girls Belmondo cut to pieces before he ran outside."

179

David J. Lake

"Poor kids," I said, thinking also of those four Earth girls who had been in *Riverhorse*. "And at the Palace?"

"We will see when we get there, but it cannot be bad. My young guards had strict orders to secure all lasers, but not to use any—nor to injure any woman. Your Queen has been a great help."

"What—Sally?"

"Yes—Sally! She gets about the palace a lot, Tom, and she suspected something already this afternoon. Not about *Riverhorse*, but about the business on the ground. She told us to go ahead—if necessary we could hold the Earthwomen in the Palace as hostages—including herself, I might say—and then the *Riverhorse* gunners would never dare to blast us. She has a cool head, your wife."

"Why didn't she tell me?" I said sulkily, as we jetted away from the ground.

"You had always the same problem, you Earthfolk who were friends of ours," he said: "none of you knew how far each of you would go. That was why we could never organize you as a party. But let us hope all this nightmare is coming to an end."

It was. When we reached the Palace roof we found a crowd of welcomers—both Earthfolk and Xumans. The only difference between them was that the Xuman guards now held the lasers. Sally, still wearing her crown, was in command of the guards; and Dave and Rosa and Sheila and Jack were talking to the Earth folk, explaining, calming.

"How many dead?" I shouted.

"Only four men," cried Sally, "including Mannheim. None wounded. There were six men and four girls in *Riverhorse*."

"And seven guys in the Fort," I said. "Twenty-one altogether. All dead: no wounded."

"It might have been worse," said Sally, "very much worse."

"Throw in all the guns here," said Varan. . . . "All right—now you will have to send a thapal-carriage to pick us up near the balloonport."

We flew back from there with all the lasers on board. Beyond Yel Karagor, the Gate of Dragons, the suburb

180

was faintly visible only by the light of star-worm lamps: the other landers and the S/Vs had burnt themselves out. Once we were over the blackness of open fields, I drew a deep breath.

"I hope the mechanism works," I said.

"If not," said Varan, "our deaths might be regarded as an atonement."

"Ha ha, very heroic," I said, "very noble. But I'd rather be ignoble and survive."

Well, I fixed that ship so none of the overrides would work, then I aimed her at the ground in a power-dive, then I pressed the ejector button.

We got ejected all right, and I could see Varan's chute open in the moonlight. Then there was an almighty explosion as the lander hit the ground. Flame exploded every which way. It looked quite pretty as I sailed down to a cold muddy landing.

And that's how we two—Varan the Hero and yours truly, Tom Carson—bombed us intrepid interstellar colonizers back into the Stone Age.

Chapter Twelve

And now I've got to admit that there was one unsuspected joker lurking in the hand I had dealt myself. A joker, or a joke—and the joke was on me. But I'll come to that later.

The first thing that hit us hard after the Midwinter Revolution was—the lack of modern transport. Suddenly relays of thapals were the fastest thing on Xuma. Instead of landers we had balloons (only east to west) and instead of S/Vs we had thapal-drawn coaches. At once the "little" planet became enormously big. It took Kanyo, for example, *two months* (48 days) to make it back to Yélsai, even though he left Svityol right after that historic "space shot," because he had to go west by gola to West Sector, and from there work his way by surface transport round the southern shore of Laral Xul. As for us in Yelsai, we'd got out of the habit of riding in coaches, and now we had to get back into that habit again—and learn a lot of other new habits.

Such as—not owning the place any more. Well, I didn't mind that; and since the Revolution had killed off the hard core of the Mannheim-Belmondo gang, people who felt like me were now in a majority.

It made things easier that the Xumans behaved very generously to us. They did just what Varan had promised—treated us as equals and fellow citizens. They even kept Sally on as Queen.

I had slept most of the Day of the New Sun. The following morning, when I woke, I found Sally had left the room, but Varan was squatting by my bedside. We got to talking about the political situation.

"Of course Sally is Queen," said Varan. "She was chosen by the *Xuman* boys, the authentic Selectors." He smiled. "It is true that via the tula from Xarth I put them up to that, but let us call that legitimate electioneering. The boys of Yelsai chose her. She must therefore remain their Queen until her change."

I yelped, "But human women don't *change*!"

"Sally says there is a—shall we say, an analog? Your women don't lose their sex, but after a time they lose the power to breed. We have put that to the Council already, and they have come up with a ruling. Because the process is much less dramatic in humans, it seemed best to have a fixed age of retirement for any future human Queens of Yelsai: four dozen and eight Xuman years. That means Sally will reign for the next twenty years, Tom, unless she abdicates first. I hope she will not abdicate: she has said she will not."

Well, there it was. Of course, one of the first acts of Queen Sally's reign was to junk the gerrymandered constitution. The Queen's Council was remodelled: the fifteen humans were expelled, and instead, in addition to the twelve old Ladies we got ten Xuman boys— mostly young guardsmen—plus one kurar and one kynthi formerly of the House of the Spring Fire-fish. This was meant to be a rough proportional representation of the adult citizens. Later on the Council planned to throw membership open to anyone, irrespective of sex group or even species. Of course, even without a single human on the Council, we invaders were still wildly over-represented in Yelsai, in the person of Sally. But the locals seemed not to mind that; they could trust Sally not to favor us unduly.

She didn't. One of her early Acts in Council—she had to talk the Xumans round on this one—was to fix a

time limit on the subsidies that we were drawing from
the State exchequer. After one more Xuman year, no
more handouts: we had to get jobs just like our red-
skinned fellows. It didn't seem that most of us were going to have town palaces and country manors after all.
Those of us who were experts on agriculture, or who
were willing to develop that skill—well, we could find a
nearby *thon* and become ordinary dirt farmers. Others
could take up various trades in the city.

And people soon began to—long before supply of
gold pieces dried up. The quickest off the mark were
some of the girls.

As things were now, we obviously were more women
than men—46 to 33, to be precise. The unlucky thir-
teen extra women, I'm happy to say, bore me surprisingly little grudge for my part in helping to kill off their
boyfriends—perhaps because they were rather tired of
their boyfriends by the time the killing happened.
Sally's Council passed a special law allowing bigamy
among members of the species *Homo sapiens* only in
the current generation: but so far there have been no
official double marriages, and several girls seem quite
happy to be on their own. Working girls they are, too.

Belmondo's ex-woman set the precedent. She had
worked at the House of the Fire-fish once before, on a
certain memorable occasion. Well, she now got herself
taken on the permanent staff—as a dancer, Xuman
style. The locals quite liked her, and with the help of
expert instructors she soon became quite skilled. Sometimes she would dance redded up, sometimes not. She
was, and is, quite a wow whether painted or plain.

Other girls now sell jewels in the Market of the
Whirling Stars. The merchants find they are good for
trade, since they have a certain novelty-value, and tourists from other cities especially like to buy from them.
(There are stories that they are engaged in another
trade, too, after market hours. If there's anything in
this, then I guess some Xuman tourist men are being
had—and the girls are not.)

We did have a problem with some of our men, the
scientists and technicians, especially those with skills in
hardware of certain sorts. A, they didn't take kindly to

the idea of getting their hands dirty, and B, they were a potential threat to the planetary status quo. The Supreme Council of Poetry solved this one by making them honorary Elders of a new Order—the Order of the Black Robe. They and their womenfolk were henceforth struck off the list of citizens of Yelsai, and were taken care of financially by Khadan. They went into monasteries (but of course with no ban on their sex lives), and got spread out over the planet. Quite a few went to Khadan itself. They are quite comfortable, I think, but possibly a bit frustrated: they spend their time urging the grey-skins to develop some basic invention like automobiles or TV, and all the time they get the story, "No, we considered that device one million years ago" (or it might be, two million) "and we decided it was not in the best interests of people." Khadan has even confiscated our radios, and now for long-distance messages we have to go to the nearest monastery, to the secluded telegraph room, and persuade the elder in charge that our use of the tula is in the planetary interest . . .

And now for my punch line. No, wait a bit: I'd better approach that more deviously. There are one or two other matters to explain first.

I put together the early part of this account from tapes that were lying around the Palace penthouse before we lost our tape recorders, plus some Xuman materials furnished by Kanyo; the rest (all but this present chapter) I got down on a dicto before the Elders impounded *that*. This last bit I'm having to *write by hand,* a skill I've had to learn lately. (I am still better at it in Xuman than in English—but then Xuman has a superbly designed cursive alphabet.)

I'm writing this in the year '0-8-7, Seventh Month, which is over two Xuman years, a little under two Earth years, since the Revolution. At that, I suppose I could drop Earth-types measures from now on, since all of you who read this will be Xumans of one type or another—even we white-skins are Xumans now. I myself have long got used to thinking in *feet* and *miles* instead of meters and kilos, and I count in duodecimals. I think it quite normal that a month is two-dozen days, and a man is one fathom tall, and a woman bears a baby in eleven months, not nine.

Talking of babies . . . Queen Sali (to use the Xuman spelling) gave birth to a fine healthy *dinoy* prince in the fall of '0-8-6. There was quite a crop of human births that season, come to that. The natives—I mean the redskins—were fascinated when they saw the little white veps; and especially they admired the babies' sexual apparatus.

"So *manly*," said Saimo, when she saw our little one. She had just given birth to her first child, too, but of course it was the usual *it*, quite smooth between the legs. She laughed. "He is sure to be a hero, like his father."

"A *hero*?" I said. "Angel, you've got me wrong . . ."

"No, I haven't," she said. "Varan has told me everything—not only about what you did in the Revolution, but also how well you are coming along now in your training."

I nearly blushed then, and I blush now to admit it, but—what I was training in was *sword fighting*. Varan and his young guards have put me through it, and now I have passed my grades as Warrior, First Class. I will never be the best swordsman on Xuma, or even in Yelsai—you have to begin your training as a vep for that—but I can defend myself. Enough to qualify for the job for which I draw my pay from the city of Yelsai.

Punchline—for services rendered, and for some alleged signs of strategic ability, I now have a title: *Warlord of Yelsai.*

One angle I hadn't quite considered when I joined Varan on the hectic night of the Revolution, and drove that last landing ship at full speed into the Xuman earth, was that I was restoring the Heroic Age on the planet. The only really modern weapon on Xuma is an immovable, half-ruined spaceship two and a half million years old, with its terrible super-laser cannon pointing vertically up at the equatorial sky. This is kept manned now by the Elders, and I suspect that any future space ship from the Solar System will be vaporized on first approach as soon as it crosses the zenith of

Svityol—but there won't be any more ships coming out of that system. Meanwhile, over at least the Middle and East Sectors, our planet is still divided into city-states, and national rivalries abound. Nakaan seems to have stopped being grateful to Yelsai for the liberation from Xarth, and the Nine Ladies of Tlanash are less friendly than they were. We still have to conscript our boys, and keep our swords sharp, and watch out for marauding balloons coming out of the east . . .

Being Warlord of Yelsai is no sinecure. I am glad the Prince of Xarth is my friend, and the staunch ally of our city.

Incidentally, Sally and I resisted the temptation to call our firstborn Carthoris! He is called Danyel, which by coincidence is a Xuman name that sounds like an Earthly one—in fact the name of my grandfather, the fighting Englishman. Danyel will have to be a warrior when he is grown up—it is the way of Xuma. At least, I am glad he will not have to face *radium rifles* (an old literary term for lasers) or *flying battleships* (i.e. landers)—but only swords and golas. By the same token, I am glad there is no chance of my becoming Warlord of *Xuma*—i.e. having to lead the planet against some interstellar enemy. I am firmly convinced that there are no space-travelling races in this far-out fringe of the galaxy apart from a few shiploads of desperate Earthmen—and Svityol will take care of those.

A week ago, on the occasion of the Spring Festival, Queen Sally gave a little party for our special friends. The Spring Festival is by tradition a country one, so we celebrated it at our little place on West Canal, Thon 1-2, just a bit north of the city oasis. Our villa slopes up a rise on the east side of the canal, and there is a nice view down to the canal bank and across to the beginnings of the Western Desert. The thon itself is not far away, and there is plenty of serious farming going on round about. Dave and Rosa, and Jack and Sheila, have all settled in this thon—the Weisers are farmers, the Willises as canal technicians. We had them along for the celebration, of course, plus many native friends. Varan and Saimo were visiting from Xarth, and from

Yelsai we had Kanyo and Psyl. (Alas, Telesin is still in Khadan.)

In the afternoon, the villa seemed to be swarming with people of all sex groups and both species. Our servants were vep-children from the thon, and many of the guests were their parents. The Mayoress and her two husbands, the local Abbot, the kurar Captain of the village guard . . . and also the exotics: an envoy from the friendly West Sector, a couple of proud Xarthian nobles of Varan's train, and some jewel-seller girls from Yelsai, both red and white. Looking at them all, I wondered: what will Xuma be like in our children's children's time? When the white species begins to increase and multiply . . . A fascinating problem.

Kanyo stood beside me, gazing at the throng.

"It is good, Lord Tomass—that there is life and peace here now." He had seemed graver, more aged since the Revolution, but now he looked better. I knew it had cost him something to launch that dark divine fire that night in Svityol. He continued:

"Killing and giving life—they are two roles, and both are necessary, but I know which is pleasanter! Of course all worlds are dying, in one sense, but now for Xuma there is hope of rebirth. Did you know, Tomass, it is calculated in Khadan that the humidity of our planet is *increasing*? In a few thousand years the oceans may begin to fill again, and rivers to flow." He smiled. "If so, our descendants may have to take countermeasures—we can't allow Svityol to be submerged. And meanwhile, let us enjoy our lovely canals."

"Yes, sure," I said.

We gathered in the garden about sunset, when the warm light lent our yellow house walls a rich reflected glory. This is the best time to watch the mating of the Fire-fish. As the sky-glow fades in the west, the streaks of fire in the canal become really fantastic. It is also the custom to launch little boats made of tula leaf on the canal, and see which way they drift, for this is the time of year for the turn-around of the waters. If they drift north, it means the season is well advanced, and the harvest will be a good one.

We launched our boats, and they drifted—north.

Everyone was very happy, not only because of the good omen, but because the weather was perfect. It was warm for the time of year, but not too hot—especially as we former invaders had all taken to Xuman dress. I had on a kilt, and the ladies, white as well as red, were in open-fronted Yelsai gowns (Sally looked lovely in that style, I may say). As the sunset faded, the stars and the Ring shone out brightly, but we did not see the star called the Toe-of-the-Hamlor, because that is in the morning sky during our spring.

"I don't care if we never see it again," said Sally. "It was a mad, bad world, and we were really mad and bad to come bursting out of it like that."

"Yes," said Psyl soberly, gazing out at the sunset. "These thin regions of space are not for travelling through, except for truly immortal gods. Little short-lived creatures like ourselves—humans or Xumans—we would do better to cultivate our own canals, as the saying goes. You can only traverse starry space, you humans, if you are willing to leave the rest of humanity behind: and the same would be true of us; and therefore we have never, ever considered it. Besides, if you did cast off into the vastnesses of space, you might stir up the real space-travellers—the gods, or the demons."

Sally shuddered. "Let's hope the various star ships have not gone far enough to do that. Twenty-odd light years was the farthest any expedition was planned for, wasn't it, Tom? We were the farthest out of all."

"We sure were crazy," said Dave Weiser, "to look for a toehold on the sky . . . but I'm glad in a way we did it. Just for ourselves, I mean. If we hadn't, we'd all be dead now. Now, there's a chance for us humans."

At least, I think he said "humans." But, come to that, maybe the word was "Xumans," after all.

And now, I don't think it makes a damn bit of difference.

ALAN BURT AKERS—

the great novels of Dray Prescot

The Delian Cycle